THE EIGHTH DAY O

&

KILLING THE SECO

Marek Hlasko was born in Warsaw in 1934.
Forced to work from an early age, he had little
formal education and left school at sixteen. At
the age of twenty Hlasko burst on the Polish
literary scene and soon became an immensely
popular figure: the 'Polish James Dean'. His
first novel, *The Eighth Day of the Week*, caused a
sensation on publication in 1956, receiving
lavish praise at home and abroad. In 1957
Hlasko was awarded the prestigious State
Publishers' literary prize for a collection of
stories, *A First Step in the Clouds*. In 1958,
however, acclaim in Poland turned to
increasingly strident criticism. *The Eighth Day
of the Week* was banned and Hlasko, denounced
as 'a decadent dabbler in literary carrion', went
into exile in the West. After a brief sojourn in
France, where his novels *The Graveyard* and
Next Stop – Paradise were published in the
emigré journal *Kultura*, he journeyed restlessly
through Europe, Israel and the United States
for the next ten years, working as a truck driver,
a manual labourer and a pimp. Between 1962
and 1964 he wrote four short novels about his
experiences in Israel, including *Killing the
Second Dog*. Marek Hlasko died in West
Germany in 1969 from an overdose of sleeping
pills. He was thirty-five.

THE EIGHTH DAY
OF THE WEEK
&
KILLING
THE SECOND DOG

Marek Hlasko

Translated by
Norbert Guterman
and Tomasz Mirkowicz

Minerva

A Minerva Paperback
THE EIGHTH DAY OF THE WEEK
& KILLING THE SECOND DOG

First published in Great Britain 1991
by Martin Secker & Warburg Limited
This Minerva edition published 1992
by Mandarin Paperbacks
Michelin House, 81 Fulham Road, London sw3 6rb

Minerva is an imprint of the Octopus Publishing Group,
a division of Reed International Books Limited

The Eighth Day of the Week first published in Poland
as *Osmy Dzien Tygodnia* copyright © 1958, 1990
by Verlag Kiepenheuer & Witsch, Koln
Killing the Second Dog copyright © 1965
by Verlag Kiepenheuer & Witsch, Koln
Translation copyright © 1990 Cane Hill Press

A CIP catalogue record for this title
is available from the British Library

ISBN 0 7493 9196 0

Typeset by Saxon Printing Ltd, Derby

Printed and bound in Great Britain
by Cox & Wyman Ltd, Reading, Berks

THE EIGHTH DAY
OF THE WEEK

1

'No,' Agnieszka said. Firmly, she pushed his hand away, and drew her skirt tight around her. 'Not now.'

'Have it your way,' the man said. He lay beside her on the grass, staring at the opposite bank of the Vistula. In the middle of the river, a comical tugboat was laboriously towing three heavy barges, its engine pumping as hard as an old man's heart. Night was falling, the cold air solidifying like milk. The trees drew darker. The man lay motionless until he felt Agnieszka's hand on his head.

'Pietrek, I don't want this to be cheap,' she said quietly. 'If I didn't love you, perhaps I wouldn't care. People might come along. I don't want others walking all over something that's important to me. You've got to understand. If there's anything we have to protect, surely it's this.'

He raised himself on his elbows, and lifted his face. She had to close her eyes: his youthful features, pure as a child's, were twisted with pain.

'Agnieszka, do you know how terrible it is to beg for it?' he said. 'Do you know what it means to wait?'

'I'm waiting too.'

He grasped her hand. His eyes were now close to hers – they were dark and had a fixed expression. 'How long must we wait? It's hell.'

'We must wait,' she said, averting her eyes. The tugboat had now been swallowed up in the mist. 'Maybe we can get an apartment. In the summer we could go away . . . You don't want it to be in some shabby room or on a park bench, do you?'

'No.'

They fell silent. Over their heads the sky was turning golden; the river too was gold. Drops of dew had appeared on the grass, and though they were sitting on his leather jacket, Agnieszka shivered. The opposite bank disappeared in the gloom.

'I've been lying,' Agnieszka said suddenly, and he detected a note of suffering in her voice. 'I can't wait any longer. I don't care. But at least try to get a room, four walls. Anything – but not here. Not in public. Do you understand?'

'Yes,' he whispered. He touched her hand: it was icy, closed like a shell. He sighed and said, 'Let's go. It's dark.'

They rose. They went through the entire Bielany Woods in silence; only when they reached the streetcar tracks, did he say, 'I'll speak to Roman, he's got a room. Let him go somewhere else for one night.'

'You'll speak to Roman,' she thought. 'I know what you'll tell him. You won't tell him that you love me and that I love you. You'll say to him, "Roman, I've got a girl, I need a place to do it. Lend me your room for one night." And he'll ask, "I hope, at least, she's pretty?"'

4

You'll make a face, and wink, and say, "How do I know? It's off-season, so what am I to do?" You won't say anything, for you too want to protect this thing. And then both of you will make a few other dirty remarks, even though you've had pitifully few women, and know absolutely nothing about them.'

There were only a few passengers in the streetcar – two old women, a sad-faced soldier, and a couple of teenage boys with a football. The lighted houses sped backwards into the dark. Agnieszka smiled and pressed close to Piotr.

'All right, Pietrek,' she said. 'Speak to Roman.'

'What's today?' he wondered aloud. 'Thursday?'

'Yes, Thursday.'

'I'll ask him to go somewhere else for Saturday night.' He touched her ear with his lips. 'So long, Agnieszka.'

The streetcar stopped. The conductor looked over his glasses and announced through his nose: 'Railway crossing.' Pietrek squeezed Agnieszka's hand and jumped out. She followed him with her eyes: he was as slender and lithe as a hazel wand. He walked with his head down. 'Why does he stoop like that?' she thought. 'My God, suppose he doesn't speak to him, after all.' After a moment he was lost in the evening crowd. The first stars were just beginning to emerge over the city; only the North Star, in the very middle of the sky, gleamed fully and steadily.

'Targowa Street,' the conductor announced. She raised her coat collar: a warm rain was beginning to fall. Two men in working clothes were walking ahead of her. One of them swore, saying to the other, 'It's pouring again. It's a long time since we've had such a filthy May. You can't even take a girl into the bushes.'

'Who for instance?' the other said. 'My mother-in-law, maybe. Got any money?' When Agnieszka passed them, he jostled her with his elbow and said to his companion, 'Would you do it with her?' 'I wouldn't mind,' the first said, 'but she won't give it to blokes like us.' 'Maybe we should ask?' the other said, and he cried, 'Hey, I'll go with you . . .'

She left them behind, and turned into Brzeska Street. Drunks were reeling in the murky circles of light under the street lamps. A drunk was bounced out of the Sailors'' Haven bar and fell on his face on the pavement: a moment later his hat and briefcase were flung out after him. Small groups stood gaping in the doorways without a word; a bass voice was blaring over a loudspeaker: 'Today's sprint ended with the defeat of the Polish team. The first to reach the goal was the Rumanian Dumitrescu . . .' From the market came the stench of rotting vegetables. Someone was singing in a shrill tenor. A young boy looked into Agnieszka's face and whistled. Another one murmured wistfully, 'Christ, she'd screw like a dream.' Cats roamed about her feet; the stars vanished in the mist. A drunk whispered hotly into her ear, 'The old lady's out of town. I have the place to myself. I'll give you some nylons, how about it?' At the East Station locomotives were tooting; only with difficulty could she get the damp air into her lungs; the faces of the passers-by were sweaty and their eyes were glazed.

'Do speak to him,' Agnieszka said to herself. 'Speak to him as soon as possible.'

2

At home her father asked her, 'Where have you been, Agnieszka?'

He was standing by the window, looking at the street through a crack between the curtains; he could stand thus for hours on end watching what was going on outside. He was short, balding, older than his years; he had an unhealthy complexion and faded eyes. He was an inspector in a co-operative union; the only times he came to life were when he managed to uncover some malpractice.

'I went for a walk,' Agnieszka said. She took off her raincoat and hung it in the hall. Then she came back. 'Has anyone been to see Grzegorz?'

'No,' her father said, continuing to drum on the window with his fingers.

'Do you believe her, that she went for a walk?' the mother asked jeeringly from her bed. She would lie for days at a time, an unattractive, soured woman, with a tendency to hysteria and a weak heart. 'Do you believe it?' she repeated. 'I bet she's been out fooling with some fellow.' She turned her perennially swollen, pale face to

Agnieszka. 'You'll get what's coming to you,' she said in an aching voice. 'But I don't want a kid here.'

'You didn't ask me if I wanted to be born,' said Agnieszka. She lit her night lamp, took out some books, and sat on her bed in the corner with her legs pulled under her, and her chin on her fists. 'I want to study,' she said.

'Study, study,' her mother said with a groan, her face wearing an expression of martyrdom. 'Grzegorz studied too, and what came of it? You'll end up like him, if you don't come to your senses.'

'I'm of age.'

'But I feed you,' her mother said. Her voice was tearful now, and her husband turned away. 'I'm the one that feeds you, nobody else,' she repeated.

'The way you cook,' said Agnieszka, 'you shouldn't mention it. Now let me study.'

'Agnieszka, Agnieszka,' her father said. His voice had no body, and now, when he tried to speak severely, he only sounded ridiculous. He wrung his hands, and looked at her reproachfully. 'How can you talk back to your mother that way? Your mother who brought you into the world.'

'Are you sure the world is so beautiful that I should be thankful to her?' Agnieszka said. She rose, throwing her books down with a thud. She walked over to the window and stood next to her father. 'I wish there were no drunks, no streets like this, and . . .'

'And what?' her mother asked aggressively.

'That's easy: no people like you.' She turned to her father. 'Has Zawadzki come back?'

'No,' her father said. He hunched up, gazing at Agnieszka with the eyes of a dog. 'He comes home late, you know.'

'I'll study in the kitchen,' said Agnieszka. She gathered up her books and walked to the door. Before going out she stopped. 'I'm sorry, Mother,' she said slowly. 'Sometimes my tongue runs away with me, and then I'm sorry.'

'Better watch out for yourself,' her mother said. She gave another groan. 'I'm sure you're going out with some good-for-nothing, when you should be staying at home.' She began to speak faster and with emphasis, 'But I'm not going to set up a nursery here – merciful Jesus, who could have foreseen all this?. . .'

Agnieszka gazed at her in silence, and walked out. She went into the kitchen and turned on the light. The kitchen was small and cluttered; the beds took up a great deal of room. One belonged to her brother Grzegorz, the other to Zawadzki, a mechanic employed by the Warsaw Gas Works, who had been staying with them since 1945, still waiting for an apartment of his own.

She sat at the table and spread out her books. With an effort she read half a page, then her father came into the kitchen. He stood in the middle of the room and cleared his throat, shifting his weight from one foot to the other. She looked at him questioningly.

'Agnieszka, what's the matter with you?' he said.

'What do you mean?'

'What's Mother talking about?'

'It's obvious. I'm a streetwalker. Tell Mother I said so. Is that enough for you?'

'Agnieszka,' her father said imploringly. 'Agnieszka . . .' He looked at her helplessly. 'I'm afraid Grzegorz will come to a bad end.' He spread his hands. 'Why don't we understand each other at all?'

'We understand each other perfectly,' said Agnieszka. 'The poor woman's sick, the apartment's small, you earn practically nothing. And now go back to the living-room, otherwise Mother will suspect you of plotting something horrible with me.'

He was sitting down now. He folded his hands on his knees, gazed at them pensively, then raised his head.

'I'm getting old,' he said. 'Sometimes I feel terribly tired. Mother's always sick, Grzegorz drinks, and you're so strange . . .' He smiled at her timidly. 'I'd like to know how you are getting along,' he said. 'Can I help you somehow?'

'No one can be helped, really helped,' she said. She pushed back her heavy bronze hair and was silent for a while. She saw that he was staring at her fixedly. 'Each of us has to help himself,' she said. 'Anything else?'

He sighed.

'Next Sunday I'll go fishing,' he said. 'I want to relax a bit, and I can't do it here. I've got my rods ready; now I still have to get a line, and that's not easy these days. Shall I go to Piaseczno? Or where I was last year, out by Wolomin? There are marl pits there.' He gave another sigh. 'It's still a long time till Sunday.'

'Three days,' she said. 'That's not much.'

'Three days,' he echoed her. He smiled. 'My God, three days. You can't imagine how many things can happen in three days. It's a terribly long time.'

'What's three days compared to a whole lifetime?'

'A great deal. Sometimes you can lose everything in three days.'

'I don't think so, but never mind. Take my advice, go back to Mother.'

He rose. 'So where should I go, Agnieszka? To Piaseczno or Wolomin?' He gazed at her intently.

'To Wolomin, of course.'

'I think that's what I'll do,' he murmured. 'Thanks.'

He walked out. It was stuffy: Agnieszka opened the window. After the rain the air was as pure as a child's breath. The street was not yet asleep. Almost all the windows were open, and from almost all of them came the nasal tones of the loudspeaker: 'With justifiable pride it must be emphasized that we have won a victory in our struggle against the cult of the individual, so harmful in its consequences, so conducive to deviations. Now we must proceed to cut it out by the roots. The directives of the Twentieth Congress must become . . .'

'If it were possible to forget,' she thought, covering her face with her hands, 'if it were possible to forget all that. Peace. A little peace and quiet. Nothing more. No Pietrek, no Father, no Grzegorz. Just peace and quiet. Let anything go on elsewhere, but where I am, let there be only peace and quiet. That is all, yes, that is absolutely all . . .'

She raised her head and again looked over to the opposite side of the street. In a window on the second floor a fat man in an undershirt was shaving, his lips twisted comically. The radio was blaring: 'Then night will come, which is our destiny.' A tractor passed,

11 of page 11

11

making a monstrous noise. Someone came into the kitchen, and Agnieszka turned. It was Zawadzki, a man in his thirties with a healthy complexion and blue eyes. His coloured shirt was unbuttoned down his chest; his neck was hard and strong.

'Good evening,' he said. He took off his coat and hung it carefully on a chair. He poured water into the basin and began to roll up his sleeves; his arms were deeply tanned.

'Going out?' asked Agnieszka.

'That's the thing to do,' he said cheerfully. 'No point in staying at home on such a fine night. How about you?'

'I have to study,' she said. 'That's why I've invaded your stronghold. The parents argue all the time.'

'What else have they got to do?' he said, grinning. 'At their age all they can do is either quarrel or play chess.' He rubbed himself with the towel so hard that his body took on the colour of freshly baked bread. 'Buy them a chess set,' he said, 'and you'll have peace and quiet at home.'

'Where are you off to?' she asked. She wished he would go now.

'To my friend's. We'll finish our work on that engine.'

'That motorcycle of yours!' Agnieszka said, smiling. 'It's all you talk about. Some day I'd like to see you ride it.'

'I have to change the clutch,' he said with some irritation. He threw down the towel, sat on his bed, and proceeded to change his shoes. For a moment he struggled with a shoelace, then raised his head. 'You wouldn't be so sharp either if you had to put up with the same rider for ten years. Do you think you're smarter

12

than my engine? I'll fix the clutch, and on Sunday I'll go to visit my fiancée.'

'Don't get angry. You've been saying that for the past three weeks.' She sat on the windowsill, swinging her legs. 'I'm curious to see what will happen then.'

'Listen, Agnieszka,' Zawadzki said. 'If they're writing me the truth, if it's true that she's betraying me, I'll fix her face so that no hospital will admit her.'

'And then?'

'I don't know.'

'Do you love her?'

'More than you think.'

'Then why do such a stupid thing?'

'Because.'

'If you didn't love her, what would you do?'

'That's easy: I'd go on living with her.'

'So what good will it do you?'

'A great deal.'

She shrugged, and leaned out of the window. People were brawling on the street in front of the entrance to a shop. 'I'll show you who's got a brother in the secret police!' someone roared. The sky looked into Agnieszka's eyes with two faces – its own and that of the puddles; both above and below, the stars were tiny, unreal. Agnieszka started: Zawadzki had put his hand on her arm. She looked at him and only now noticed for the first time that the man standing before her had a bitter mouth, and that there were hard lines on his forehead.

'Listen,' he said. 'All of you are basically the same, and that's why there's actually no point talking to you. But I'll tell you one thing: a man wants to have something for

13

himself alone, and you can't change that. If he can't have a friend or a girl like you, he wants at least to preserve his beggarly sense of honour. When we were at the Oflag, one of our boys got a letter from his family saying that his girl was going out with Germans. We were so bored in the camp that everybody teased the boy mercilessly. "It's nothing, Mietek," we told him, "don't take it so hard. After you go back home and marry her, hang a print of the *Battle of Grunwald* over your bed. You'll feel better whenever you look at it: that time, *we* beat *them*." The boy was going wild from frustration. Finally he said, "Never mind, I'll teach her a lesson." "And what if this is another Thirty Years'' War?" "I'll take care of her in two weeks," he said, and next day he was gone. We covered up for him for a month, and then he came back. "I've done it," he said. Well, Agnieszka, he crossed three borders twice, because he had to go a roundabout way, for the sole purpose of killing her. He did it with a broken bottle – you can imagine. He was a madman, that's certain, but I liked him better than some I've known.'

He walked away from her. He took a coat from the closet and put it on.

'What became of him?' Agnieszka asked.

'That boy, you mean?'

'Yes.'

Zawadzki's smile wasn't pleasant. 'Well,' he said, 'he got no pleasure from what he'd done. After all, he might have got a gun and put an end to her. He seemed to have lost his mind. He walked about the camp saying, "I satisfied her for life." In the end he cut his throat with a

14

razor in the latrine. Good night, Agnieszka. Where's Grzegorz?'

'I don't know,' said Agnieszka. 'Must be drinking somewhere.'

'Is her still waiting for her?'

'Still.'

'That, too, is a fine thing,' said Zawadzki. 'Good night.'

He walked out; his steps echoed loudly on the stairs – he took several steps at a time, like a little boy. The street brawl was ending. The drunks now had their arms around each other. 'And why do you do such things to me, Witek?' one of them blubbered. He had a young voice. 'That's life,' the other one said. 'In that case, everything's all right,' a third man concluded. He drew them to him and introduced them to each other. 'Get acquainted, gentlemen: an old army pal – a school pal.' 'Ah,' said the first and began to giggle. 'Ah . . .' Arm in arm the three of them stamped out the stars in the puddles.

'The end,' Agnieszka thought. She closed the window and sat at the table.

Her father came into the kitchen. He was wearing a motley costume – an old homespun topcoat, a dark hat, a cotton scarf. 'I'm going to get Grzegorz,' he said. 'Mother is having hysterics.'

'Where will you look for him?' Agnieszka said. She walked up to her father. She was taller than him, and seemed stronger. Next to her he looked like a dry bush alongside a sapling. She stared at him for a while, then her clear eyes suddenly went out, like a spark covered by a hand. 'You're planning to drag him out of some bar?'

'Yes,' he said. He shifted his weight from one foot to the other and put his hands behind his back. He tried to look resolute. 'I'll drag him out of his bar,' he said, 'and I'll give him such a talking-to that he'll not want another drink for a long time.'

'Stefan!' her mother cried in a weak voice. 'Are you on your way?'

'Yes, dear, I'm going,' he said. He adjusted his hat and took a step towards the door.

'Just a minute,' said Agnieszka. She walked over to the door and shut it.

'If you find him at all,' she said. She forced her father to sit on a chair, and took his hat from his hand. 'It won't be easy,' she said. 'Nor will your talk be of any help. Tomorrow he'll drink again. Don't bother him.'

'Why?'

'He's completely alone now.'

'Why?'

'He's in love.'

'But he has parents, a home, a sister.'

'He has nothing except torment.'

'What torment?'

'It's his business, not ours.'

'So I'm supposed to sit at home and wait calmly while my son is knocking about in bars!' He rose and reached for his hat. He banged his fist on the table. 'Devil take it,' he said. 'I'll bring him home if I have to drag him!'

'Home,' Agnieszka echoed. 'Home – where Mother does nothing but groan and you sit with a pencil working out that fifteen years ago you could buy sixty quarts of vodka on your pension, while now it scarcely comes to twenty. Home, where he has no corner for himself. To this day his parents can't understand how they have managed to be bored with each other for twenty-odd years! Home! Why, here there's no real difference between the crucifix and the portrait of Stalin, for none of us understands either of them. This is the home you want to bring him back to?'

He was silent. He sat motionless, his head lowered. He clasped his hands together on his knees and squeezed them so hard that they turned white, like the hands of a dead man.

'What am I to do?' he said after a moment. He reached for his hat, then put it down again. 'What am I to do?' he repeated. 'I'd like to do what's best for you.'

'Don't stoop,' she said. 'On Sunday you'll go fishing. I'll go to get Grzegorz.'

She took his hat from his hand, and went out to the hall. She put on her coat, pocketed the house keys. Her father said imploringly: 'Come back soon . . . God, I wish it were Sunday already . . .'

'If she comes for Grzegorz,' Agnieszka said, 'ask her to leave a note for him.'

'Agnieszka,' said her father, 'will she ever come?'

She stopped in the doorway. 'No.'

She walked out into the street. The sky had turned completely dark. The city was falling asleep, sprawled motionless under the sharp brilliance of the stars.

3

'He's here,' the doorman said with a smile for Agnieszka. There was a wide gap between his two front teeth, and it somehow gave his face a roguish air. 'At the bar. How will you get through to him? There's such a crowd tonight . . .' He walked away towards a noisy party of new arrivals.

Agnieszka went inside. The room was dark and stuffy; star-shaped bulbs gleamed in the low ceiling. She was obliged to stop near the dance floor; the couples crowded into a few square yards stepped on each other's feet and continually bumped into each other, apologizing and exchanging greetings. The women were all dressed alike, and all perfumed with the same cheap *Poem*. They had their heads on their partners'' shoulders, a cloud of smoke hovered under the ceiling, the curly-headed vocalist was tearfully mumbling something about separation. One of the waiters said to Agnieszka, 'Step aside please, you're in the way . . .' He looked at her face close up. He was young, handsome and dark, gleaming with brilliantine and a gold tooth. 'Yes,' she said sorrowfully, 'that's the way it is.' She smelled the alcohol on his breath as he walked away; his brilliantine was so strong that even in the smoke-filled air it left a distinct odour. The stout saxophonist, with the characteristically puffy face of musicians who have played for many years in night-clubs, was clumsily imitating American soloists. A drunken woman laughed hysterically, clinging tightly to her partner; her hands spread as though webbed, very white, with plump fingers. Agnieszka smiled bitterly. The dance ended abruptly and dozens of sweaty-faced dancers went by her on their way back to their seats. A drunk lingering on the dance floor cried, 'More!' Two women dragged him to a table. Lights were turned up; the musicians wiped their foreheads and put down their instruments.

'You look like the Mona Lisa,' someone said to Agnieszka from behind her. 'Do you have such a sad face because, like her, you have no pretty Tissot wristwatch? We might have a talk on that subject . . .'

She went on into the bar. There was a dreadful crowd; people were screaming, singing, abusing one another, clinking glasses, and exchanging kisses and handshakes. Behind the counter two barmen in white aprons ran back and forth. One was small and thin, with a mobile, cheerful face; the other was tall, and his face was impenetrably calm. He wielded his glasses with stony seriousness; in serving each customer he acted like a surgeon preparing for an operation, convinced, however, that everything would go well, according to the will of his hands and brain. He did not react at all to the desperate cries of the drinkers, working according to his own extraordinarily precise plan.

Finally she made her way to Grzegorz. He sat at the far end of the counter, where the zinc ended in a gentle curve. He looked straight ahead of him with bleary eyes, not speaking to anyone. There was a striking resemblance; like her, he was tall, with hair that could not be called definitely either dark or light; his eyes, like hers, changed colour with the weather, ranging from light blue to dark green. His face was puffy, and he had a short nose; lines around his mouth pulled it downwards. He leaned his head on his hand. When Agnieszka touched it, he started.

'Did she come?' he asked.

She shook her head. 'No,' she said. 'You're really soaking it up, Grzegorz.'

He looked at her with an empty glance as at an inanimate object. 'It's not impossible that you're right,' he said. He pulled a glass of water nearer him. 'But what inference do you draw from this?'

'I feel like having a couple of drinks with you,' she said. 'And I don't want to have to do with a dead man, like the day before yesterday. Can you buy me a drink?'

'I don't know whether I can,' he said, 'but I will.' He beckoned to the barman. 'Fill "em up,' he said in a confidential whisper. He lifted his glass and clinked it with Agnieszka's. They drank. He looked at her unseeingly. 'So she didn't come, after all,' he said. His voice sounded sober; Agnieszka realized that he was trying to get drunk but couldn't.

'No,' she said, 'she didn't come.'

He smiled. 'I know that without your telling me,' he said. 'Do you by any chance know why the devil I'm asking?'

'I know. But she didn't come.'

He nodded. The cheerful barman asked: 'Another round?' Without waiting for an answer, he quickly filled their glasses and vanished among the bottles. The orchestra struck up again; drinkers got down off their bar stools and began to elbow their way towards the dance floor.

'I knew she wouldn't come,' said Grzegorz. 'The nights are the worst, Agnieszka. I close my eyes and see her; she holds out her hands and says something to me that I can't hear or understand. It seems to me that in her home she also stares into the darkness and addresses her prayers to me just as I address my prayers to her. But when I open my eyes I see only a corner of Zawadzki's bed, and a piece of the ceiling. I hear the tap dripping. Couldn't that tap be repaired? And then I lie awake for hours. When a taxi stops in front of the house, I get up from the bed and walk over to the window. It seems to me that she will get out of the taxi, come up for me, and that all this torment will end. I count the steps on the staircase, the shadows and the voices. Will you fix that tap tomorrow?'

'Yes.'

He fell silent. He pushed their glasses over towards the barman. 'Fill them up, please,' he said. 'And some kind of water . . .'

'Hasn't he had enough?' The barman looked questioningly at Agnieszka.

She shook her head. 'Please, fill them up,' she said.

He filled the glasses and walked away. Two elderly men drank to each other. 'Here's to you. My name's Wacek, and yours?' 'Jozek.' 'Which Jozek? Pilsudski?'

'No.' 'The other one?' 'Neither. Jozio Kwiatkowski.'
'Well, cheers.' 'Cheers.' The orchestra was playing a
tango. Agnieszka lifted a corner of the curtain separating
the bar from the dance floor and watched the dancers. A
small man standing beside her said: 'I'm getting out of
this country. Here you can only be a drunk or a hero.
Normal people have nothing to do here. So long.' He
paid and walked away.

'Is today Thursday?' Grzegorz asked.

'By now it's Friday.'

'Till Sunday,' he said. 'If only I can stick it out till
Sunday. Then everything will be clear: either – or.
That's what she said: she needed one week to think it
over. Only two or three days to go. If she doesn't come
before Sunday evening, this means the end. And then
. . .'

'What then?' she asked sharply.

He raised his head and looked her straight in the eyes.
He was silent for a while. 'Then nothing,' he said. 'I'll go
on living. That's the worst of it.'

'It's not the worst when you're twenty-five,'
Agnieszka said.

He shrugged his shoulders. 'What does it prove?' he
said with an air of contempt. 'Moreover, who is twenty-
five today? And what of it? How can this knowledge help
me? I hope you won't be so stupid as to tell me that I have
my life before me, that everything is still ahead of me,
and so on. There's not a man alive who really believes
that. Every human feeling is sacred and there is no
guarantee that a man will want to be foolish for the
second time in his life and give another woman as much

22

as before, and after all that's what's in question. "To give everything." After all, that's what you call all those douches, rubber caps, and abortions, don't you?'

'Well, what then?'

'I think Slowacki has one of his characters ask, "Is the soul a lamp that never burns out?" Before every good human feeling we should kneel as before a shrine, as before a star. We should protect it, carry it like a light, and if there is even a little spark left, blow till we're out of breath. This is the twentieth century, Agnieszka: Isolde lives in a brothel, and Tristan gets drunk with the pimps at the corner bar. People today have little time for great feelings; they hop out of bed early, lap up their little soup in milk bars, squeeze into streetcars, quarrel with conductors over pennies, buy flimsy furniture in department stores on the instalment plan, and so on. To kneel,' he said, 'to kneel. Life gives no guarantees regarding the future. Everyone who says, "Give it up, in a few years something else will come along," deserves a spit in the face. What will come? When will it come? Every bit of happiness comes the bad way.'

He paused and nodded to the barman. He looked into the filled glasses after the barman had gone. A woman sitting a few stools farther along sang in a squeaky voice, 'I am so tiny . . .' 'But you can hold a lot,' said a male voice with conviction. The woman stopped singing; she bent over her glass, mumbling something unintelligible. The saxophonist was still trying to imitate American jazz. The cheerful barman cast an alert glance at Grzegorz. 'Coffee?' he said.

Grzegorz came to. 'If you say so,' he said, 'but it's a waste of effort; today I won't get drunk anyway.' He turned to Agnieszka: 'Want some coffee?' She nodded. 'Two coffees, please,' Grzegorz said. The barman came back and put two cups before them. Grzegorz tasted his and shook his head sadly. 'The coffee is lousy, too,' he said.

The cheerful barman spread his hands. 'It's the times we live in,' he said, and walked away.

'To hell with the times,' said Grzegorz. 'Another idiotic myth.' He turned to Agnieszka. 'Something occurred to me.'

'Yes?'

'I'd like to write something some day.'

'A book?'

'Yes, a book.'

'About love?'

He burst out laughing, and the lines around his eyes turned white. 'Oh, no,' he said. 'To write about love is to make yourself ridiculous. So far, at least, all love literature is nothing but glorified crap. God, what has it got to do with love? I'd like to read something about myself and my feelings when for the twentieth night in a row I can't sleep and lie staring at the ceiling. Everything written on the subject is insipid, like brass compared with the sun. Only Dostoyevsky is a little bit truthful, but you run away from his love with your hands burned, like from a red-hot iron. This isn't for modern man. Not for the times we live in.' He bent towards Agnieszka and took her hand. 'Listen,' he said, 'this will be something entirely new. The story of two people. We won't call them by their right names nor will we invent names for them.' He was slightly drunk all the same, and his speech got a bit thick; his breath was searing. He said, 'Yes, this is something entirely new. The story of two people who met at one of life's bad corners. I don't know yet who they are, I have to make up my mind, see? He must be commonplace, very commonplace; she too, probably, though I don't know . . . Let's say he drinks too much and complains, could be, no? What else was there to do during that time, except drink and gamble? In Poland drunks have a privileged status, drunkenness has become something like a new special morality. It's known that when a man drinks, something's worrying him. But never mind, let's get back to our subjects . . . And what about her? The devil knows what kind of person she ought to be. She must have been through a great deal, she must somehow be resigned or embittered. Whenever anything starts up, it's hard to believe that this time it really will be worthwhile. This customer, for instance, is out to get drunk, because he's in a hurry to destroy something in himself, he's afraid of suffering, and so on. She's running away from all that too, for to tell the truth her friend is no good, he drinks like a fish, brawls, has a stretch of bad life behind him. And yet there is something good in him, somehow, somewhere. At some point, on the seventh day, there must be something worth while, something good, and they want somehow to dig through to it, at any price. The earth is a lousy place, life is a comical little hell, but somewhere deep underneath the surface, molten metal glows white hot. And they try to build up that worthwhile thing by sheer willpower. It falls apart a thousand times each day, each hour, but they start it all over again a thousand

25

times. Perhaps everything might even turn out well in the end, who can tell? But then people begin to help them.'

He suddenly straightened himself and pushed Agnieszka's hand away. 'People,' he said. 'Bloody stupid people who never have enough of their own little hell and stick their noses into other people's hells. They begin to touch it all with their sweaty hands, to whisper, to plan, to help, to draw them aside, and to inform them about themselves. "Do you know," they tell him, "that she lived with this man and that man?" "Do you know," they say to her, "that in 1947 he murdered the station-master at Mysliborz, as well as the cashier and the assistant engineer? Do you know that he's this and she's that?" People meddle, people lie, people invent ignoble nonsense, and then one day nobody knows what's true and what's a lie, what is slander and what is reality, who is a friend and who is a pig, who is a mate and who is a bum; there's just no way of knowing what's what, and they decide to part . . .'

He stopped; his jaw muscles trembled. Now he looked pitiful. The cheerful barman glanced at him and asked, 'Fill it up?'

He nodded, then took his glass and drank it down in one gulp. Agnieszka asked, 'Is that the end?'

'Not at all,' he said without looking at her. 'That would be too simple, and after all people want to understand each other to the bitter end. But I don't know what is to come next. It's the end, obviously it's the end, but something else has to happen first. Yes, yes, I'm sure of that, but I still don't know exactly what . . . Something extraordinarily banal. This doesn't have to be a good book, why the devil should it be good? Anyway, no one will write a book about true love, such things are too terrible and too ridiculous, no one dares reveal them completely . . . What will it be then? What's needed is something banal, something stinkingly banal. Perhaps illness? Or some sort of moon, some moonlit water? Some such thing must exist, after all; you think about it too. A railway accident, a disaster, death? Death, perhaps death? When all's said and done, nothing can be more banal. And so, what kind of death, Agnieszka? Caused by the bite of a poisonous ant, by a brick dropping from some scaffolding? Perhaps suicide? But who – he or she? No, he, obviously – despite everything, women love life more than men. Yes. Now I have it.'

He paused for breath. His hair clung to his forehead, he pushed it back. His face was sweaty and swollen, his eyes had grown smaller.

'He kills himself,' Agnieszka said. 'And that's the end?'

He pondered a while. 'No,' he said, 'despite everything, it isn't the end yet. It's barely the first half, the end is still far away. The suicide doesn't come off, Agnieszka, in this story nothing can be successful. What comes later is even worse, because it turns out that the things we're scared of and blackmailed by here on earth amount to very little. But what comes later? Happy endings are never too clever in literature. They part. The end. Full stop. Maybe they'll try to live intelligently, maybe they won't, who can tell? But at this point we must put an end to it, the game is up. So they part. The pursuit of happiness is over and done with. It's always pointless, but it is worth while to sacrifice one's life for it. This isn't me, it's Stendhal. Is it worth it or isn't it?' he asked the barman.

'It is,' said the barman.

'It isn't,' said Grzegorz, 'but never mind. Two more vodkas, please.'

'She wouldn't forgive you that,' said Agnieszka.

'What?'

'What you've just said.'

'She won't come anyway.'

'Do you want to destroy everything?'

'Yes,' said Grzegorz. 'I don't want to remember anything. It's too cruel to ask a man to recall his most sacred moments. Memories are garbage.'

'What's the title of this book?' Agnieszka asked.

'Hard to tell,' he said hesitantly. 'Anyway, it will live only in my imagination. After all, I'm a chemist, damn it. As for the title – something about silence, about the need to be silent in front of others. So what should it be?'

The bar had been emptying. The cheerful barman busied himself wiping the counter with an immense rag. The espresso machine had stopped hissing, the orchestra had long been silent. Someone was asleep, his head on his arms. A friend tugged at him, saying over and over again, 'Bolek, stand up . . . Bolek, don't be drunk . . . Bolek, don't be a pain in the neck . . .'

'We're closing now,' the cheerful barman said. 'Till tomorrow.'

Grzegorz paid, and they walked out together. A chilly wind was sweeping the streets. Grzegorz bent towards Agnieszka and took her hand; his was sweaty and hot.

28

'Will she come?'

'The lovers met too late,' Agnieszka said. She yawned, she felt sleepy.

Grzegorz burst out laughing. 'Agnieszka, that's another fairy tale,' he said, letting go of her hand. 'I'm only a little older than you, but I can tell you this: I've never yet seen people who met at the right moment in life. There is no such moment in life, and there can't be. It always seems too late or too early, there is too much experience or too little. There is always something that stands in the way. This can't be important.' After a moment he asked, 'Did you like it?'

'No, I hate sadness. Silence and black colours – they're only good for the dead.'

'I won't drink any more, Agnieszka,' Grzegorz said. 'It seems to me that I love you very much. I wish you were at least a bit different.'

They stopped. The night sky was thinning out; it was dirty and full of empty clouds. The dawn clung to the damp roofs. Taxi drivers yawned, the first milk carts dragged along; someone was following them from a distance, cursing at the top of his lungs.

'I too love you very much,' said Agnieszka. 'You know yourself how much.'

4

The leaves were thick and covered the sky; lying flat on their backs they saw nothing overhead except a mass of greenery; nor could they see the singing birds. The warm grass had a bitter smell, and at ground level a low wind brought the scent of pine and the first heather. Now and then squirrels darted out of the thick undergrowth; they stared attentively with their beady little eyes, and after a while scrambled up into the branches with unbelievable speed.

'That's all I remember of my childhood.'

'A squirrel?'

'Yes. We once had a squirrel at home. It was given to me when I was ten.'

'What did you call it?'

'Joasia. It wasn't afraid at all. I slept with it, it ran after me like a puppy, and when I ate, it stuck its nose in my plate.'

'And then?'

'Joasia died. Squirrels' teeth grow too long unless they eat nuts. One day it couldn't open its mouth, and there was nothing we could do about it.'

'Why didn't you give it nuts?'

'It was during the Occupation. Mainly we ate bread and jam. As far as I know, the jam then was made of beetroot.'

'Is that really all?'

'What do you mean, all?'

'Is that all you remember?'

'Isn't it enough for you? Why remember everything?'

'Tell me.'

He shrugged his shoulders. 'The other things I'd rather not remember.'

'Are there a lot of them?'

'Enough.'

'That's strange.'

'What's strange?'

'We know so little about each other.'

'Little?'

'Terribly. Every day you're different.'

'But you don't want my memories. Every time I begin to talk you ask me to stop.'

'I want different ones.'

'But those are the most important.'

'I want you to forget those. That's the first thing I'd like to do for you. Don't remember those things, Pietrek.'

'So what is it you do want to know about me?'

'For instance, what are you thinking this minute?'

'What if it's silly?'

'Let it be. After all, one doesn't go to Bielany with Einstein. Talk.'

He put his arms around his knees. She raised his face: he had a pure profile, calm in its youthful severity.

'I'm thinking of when this torment will end, these meetings in cafés, parks, cinemas . . .' He closed his eyes, and a painful grimace formed around his mouth. 'Walls,' he said, 'four walls, Agnieszka. To be with you for a week; a day and a night together, then I could die. This is terrible: each day I spend without you is stolen from my life. How many such days have there been? How many will there be? First those years, and now this wandering . . . No one will give them back to us, no day can return. How many good days could we have had behind us? How long will it go on like this?'

'Don't talk about it, Pietrek.'

'Sometimes I don't want to believe all that,' he said. 'We're alone, completely alone, do you understand? And no one will help us, no matter how much we beg and no matter who we ask. I suppose there's no one anywhere who can give us a wall. We must wait – and that's that. We must wait and wait, a very long time, and if in the end we get what we want, we probably won't have the strength to enjoy it. We'll have lost many days of our lives unnecessarily. That's the worst.'

'Many people have no walls.'

'Many people have nothing at all. But that's no reason.'

'That's life.'

'I don't like that phrase. What does it mean, after all?'

'Everything.'

'And nothing.'

'Maybe. Now it's summer. You should go away somewhere, Pietrek. To rest.'

'And when I'm back everything will start all over again. We'll long for each other, and kiss in doorways after sunset. Then we won't sleep for nights on end, and we'll think about how we can be helped and by whom. And we'll be parting continually. We'll long for each other, torment each other, quarrel, and abuse each other. Not because we're not in love. No. Just because we have no walls. If Romeo and Juliet lived in Warsaw in the year 1956 they would probably never meet. And the worst of it is, it's nobody's fault.'

He fell silent. He stared up at the green dome of the trees, and after a moment said, 'The worst of it is I love you. With others all this would have been so easy.'

'What?'

'Everything and nothing.'

He lay flat on his back, his arms under his head. Through the thick foliage he gazed at the red sun setting. It did not take long: the woods began to grow dark, and the leaves lost their colour. Nearby was a rifle range, and the soldiers who had finished their day were coming back, singing, 'The night is so long.' They drew out the last syllable, finishing it abruptly. 'Three, four,' a voice roared, and they sang in chorus, 'It's a pity to waste it.' A sleepy breeze came from the warmed river.

'Piotr.'

'Yes.'

'Have you got that room?'

'Yes.'

'Tomorrow?'

'Yes.'

'He won't be there?'

'We'll be alone.'

'You didn't tell him that you'd come with me?'

'No.'

'What am I to say at home?'

'Best not to say anything.'

'I must. Mother'd be nervous.'

'Say that you're going out of town.'

'Where?'

'Anywhere.'

'What for?'

'Anything.'

'Think of something.'

'To Podkowa Lesna. To visit a friend. To study together for the exam. Why do you talk like that? How old are you, Agnieszka?'

'When I'm with you, I'm twenty-two. And you?'

'A hundred.'

'Why do you say that?'

'Does the date on my birth certificate matter? There are places on earth where every day is a century. One only has to get there.'

'What year were you arrested?'

'Fifty-two.'

'It won't happen again, will it?'

'If all that were to happen again, if all that had to be repeated, no one would survive . . . When I was there I thought about you, do you know?'

'Where?'

'At Mokotow.'

'You didn't know me then.'

'That's unimportant. I thought that if I got out I'd meet you. And that we'd never part, and that I'd never go back there. I died every day at sunrise, and every day I came back to life. The commander there was some colonel. He would say to us, "This is Mokotow. People who get out of here push up the daisies." At interrogations he screamed: "We'll kill you the Bolshevik way, a bullet in the back of the head . . ." Then I thought about you.'

'What has become of him now?'

'The commandant?'

'Yes.'

'He's been arrested. I read about it somewhere.'

'Does it make you happy?'

'Too late to make me happy.'

'You won't think about it ever again, will you?'

'If I didn't have you, I'd think about it all the time. Now I think you are the person given me by fate as a reward, to make up for the bad old days. Only you. But it's hard to forget, I tell you, Agnieszka. There are things one probably can't ever forget. I remember once . . .'

'Now things will be different, won't they?'

'Why do you say that all the time?'

'I must.'

'Well, then things must be different.'

'When we have a place of our own we won't let anyone inside for a year. We'll have a sign on the door, saying, "No one at home. Gone away for a year."'

'That's funny.'

'Why?'

'I was once in a cell with a man who dreamed the same thing. "After I finally get out of this charming little place," he would say, "I'll lock myself up at home and won't stick my nose outside. To hell with all that

35

cherished freedom." It seems dreams are the same on both sides of the bars.'

'What kind of furniture will we have?'

'At times no one could fall asleep,' Piotr said, and she knew at once that now he would not listen to any of the things she wanted to tell him, and that she would have to listen to him, although she knew every one of his recollections of that place. Piotr said, 'We talked in whispers. We told each other everything – delusions and facts alike. No one knew why or what for, and no one listened anyway. Everyone unreeled his own film in his own head. Each of us thought only of himself, and of his own affairs which didn't exist . . .'

'Stop talking about all that,' she said. 'Think of our home. And your son. We are going to name him Fyodor, aren't we, after Dostoyevsky . . .?'

'I recalled everything, my whole life, every single last thing that happened. I recalled every person I had ever spoken to, all the words that were spoken, every single day, every single night; finally I reached the point of trying to recall every single thought. What I thought one year, five years, ten years before. What had I done? At what moment in my life had I made the fatal blunder, the thing about which I knew nothing, about which no one would tell me anything? Had one of my friends been a spy? Had someone worked for the political police? Who was the man responsible for putting me where I now found myself? What did he look like? Was he old or young? Did he live alone or did he have a family? Where had I met him? At a bar, at school, in the street, in the sports stadium? How had it begun? And what had I talked to him about? Sometimes I would hang on in my thoughts to someone, a person who suddenly seemed he must be the man I was looking for. And then I would think: it is he, it can't be anyone else, it must be he. What had I done to him? What had he done? How had he managed to get me here? Had he done it on purpose, or had I been caught with him? I choked with hatred for him, and then somebody else would occur to me, and all over again I would try to remember where I had met him, and what he had looked like, and what I had talked to him about, and what he could have reported about me.'

'Don't think about it,' said Agnieszka. 'Don't talk about it, think what tomorrow will be like. There will be no one except us. You'll snuggle up to me. I'll hug you, and you'll stop thinking about it. You'll stop thinking about an apartment, and about the prison, and about everything that torments you. The only important thing will be us, and our few hours before daybreak. Yes?'

'Yes, Agnieszka. But who was he? Will I never know?'

'Try to think that you won't. What do you need him for? Do you want to take revenge on him?'

'No, no . . . I'd just like to look at him, if only for a second. To look at his face for one second. Nothing more. I think that if I could see him once I'd understand many things about my life. Perhaps even everything. That's what I think sometimes. And I suppose I'd give everything for it.'

'Even me?'

'Even you.'

'In that case it's a good thing that you'll never know anything about it. Now we must go.'

'So soon?'

'I want to do some studying tonight . . .'

'Agnieszka.'

'What, darling?'

'If I didn't have you, I wouldn't want to live. You are now the only thing I really believe in. You, nothing else. I suppose I have the right to think so. If I didn't have you, I'd do everything to go to pieces completely, to destroy myself, so as never to love, never to believe, and never to suffer again. Without you this side of the prison bars has no meaning for me, it would be just like the other side. Do you understand?'

'Yes. But stop talking about it. Think of tomorrow.'

'All right.'

'Promise me. Promise that you'll think only of tomorrow, that you won't even mention the other thing. All right?'

'Yes.'

'Will you take me home?'

'Why do you ask?'

They rose and walked in the direction of the streetcar. The woods were quiet, grown enormous in the dusk. The domes of the trees merged into each other and into the dark sky.

5

Brzeska Street was not yet asleep. This was the fifteenth of the month, and as always on payday, men were standing around in front of their houses. Their shirts were unbuttoned; their chests, hair, and faces glistened with sweat. Before the day had gone, its leaden sky had harrassed houses, bodies, pavements, and trees. There were those who stood and those who sat; those who walked from one end of their street to the other, from one little group to the next, from one street lamp to the next; those who lounged against the walls on patches of trampled grass; those whose dishevelled heads leaned out from dirty ground-floor windows – all were drinking: beer, vodka, and cheap wine straight from the bottle; they choked as they drank, and the liquor splashed over the sores on their hands, onto their sweaty shirts, and their soft relaxed bodies. The wind, like a tired animal, ran clumsily along the sidewalks, bearing the smell of their sweat, their tobacco, and their breath, hot and rancid with alcohol. Among them women glided to and fro, some in old dressing-gowns or with overcoats hastily thrown over their slips, others wearing brightly coloured dresses with dark half-circles of sweat under the arms;

39

some were urging the men to come back home, others to go into town for further revelling. They quarrelled with the men, drew them away from their comrades, snatched bottles out of their unwilling hands; and they reviled the men in the men's own coarse language.

Agnieszka was familiar with paydays; she knew what Saturday, Sunday, and the nights before holidays were like in this street. Each time she turned into the great buzz that filled that street from wall to peeling wall, she was overcome with fear – a stifling, heavy, and repulsively intimate fear, for she had lived with it for many years. She tried to pass by quickly, defending herself against the drunks, and pushing back the men on the make whenever she did not manage to avoid them altogether. Today she hoped she could safely run the gauntlet of all those bleary eyes.

She pressed close to Piotr and shut her eyes. They entered the street with their arms about each other. It was only a few hundred yards to the house where she lived, and at first she thought they would pass unnoticed. Then, from a doorway where several of them stood – their faces could not be seen in the dark – someone said to Piotr, 'Look out for that tail, it's loaded.'

Piotr started forward. Agnieszka held him back with all her weight. 'Don't! I beg you, don't!'

'Let go of me!'

'They'll kill you!'

She sank her nails into the palm of his hand, and with each step sank them deeper, so that she felt the pulsation of his veins. She whispered, 'If you make a move, I won't go with you, I won't, I won't.'

They walked on. Someone said, 'Why did they annoy her? I know her.'

'Is she a good girl?'

'I'm sure of it.'

'Leave her alone, you bully.'

'Hooligan, you mean. A hooligan always has it ready.'

'Baby doll!'

'Come on, just once, you could make me very happy.'

'Hello, girlie.'

'Don't be so stuck-up.'

'Looks like a real geisha.'

'Ever tried her?'

'Me? Such things aren't for me. I'm a modest man.'

'Where do you find the strength for it? Not on potatoes.'

'Don't worry. If she gave it to you, you'd do it six times.'

'In six months maybe.'

'Don't,' Agnieszka whispered, 'please, don't.'

'Do you live alone, lady?'

'I'd try her, but he won't take his hands off it.'

'A sturdy girl, Zfyszko. She'd kill you.'

'Christ, if only she'd let me!'

'Ask her, maybe she's generous.'

'She can't say no.'

'Michalowski caught the whole works from a doll just like that.'

'Syphilis?'

'Siberian chancre.'

'Don't,' whispered Agnieszka, 'don't . . .'

'Very pretty!'

'God! One shot at that, and I'd die happy.'

'I'd work at it all night.'

'Hot stuff.'

'What of it?'

'Don't get upset. There's a way for a sparrow to satisfy a mare.'

'Don't put your head down.'

'I can lift my head all right. But who'll lift that thing?'

'Does this little squirt actually screw her?'

'He must jump like a rabbit at it, going like a fiddler's elbow.'

'Can he make her come? He's so puny!'

'Ask him.'

'Hey mate, how do you do it?'

'Here, let me lend you mine!'

'Never do that. I lent mine to a friend for his wedding once, and look what he gave me back.'

'I'm looking. I don't see anything.'

'That's the point.'

'Ask her how much she wants.'

'How much have you got?'

'Twenty zlotys.'

'You know what you can do with your twenty zlotys.'

They turned into the doorway. It was dark, and they blessed the darkness. The street was silent now, and they could hear only their own feverish breathing. Agnieszka leaned heavily against the wall, they had to catch their breath. Her face stood out against the wall, a pale spot. He saw the terrible look in her eyes. There was a smell of urine and of laundry coming from one of the upper floors. A lorry rumbled by, cats were serenading each other. Pietrek said hoarsely, 'Nothing happened, nothing. There was only the woods, there is only tomorrow. Do you hear me?'

He tried to take her hand, but she wrested herself free. She was silent and again he could only hear her rapid breathing. In the janitor's room the radio sang hoarsely: 'I shall walk along a silvery path among the gardens . . .' Someone abruptly turned it off; and once again there was only silence punctuated by the cats screaming.

'Nothing happened,' Piotr repeated. 'Tomorrow at this time we'll be together, tomorrow at this hour . . .'

He stretched out his hands towards her head. Then, with all her strength she struck his face with her fist. He reeled, stumbled against a box lying on the ground, and fell. His head hitting the concrete made a hard sound.

'Go away,' she cried. 'Go away, go!'

Without looking back, quickly, taking three steps at a time, she ran upstairs.

6

Once in the flat, she hung up her overcoat and went into the living-room, almost unconscious, shaking all over. Her father was walking on his hands. His shirt had slid out of his trousers. His face was swollen from the effort, his eyes were bloodshot, he breathed heavily, drops of sweat rolled down his bald pate; the spectacle was repulsive, and Agnieszka averted her eyes. This mania of her father's she found particularly revolting, although she pitied him a little. When he saw her, he performed an adroit somersault, and stood up in front of her, beaming with satisfaction.

'I've still got some strength, eh?' he asked.

'Probably a good deal.'

'You young people have no idea,' he said, 'what a splendid thing physical strength is. Sometimes, looking at those weaklings, I feel sorry for them: today's men are as feeble as stewed spiders.' He took his upper plate out of the glass and put it smartly into place. He was still flexing his muscles: they looked hard and round, running like little mice under his faded skin. He lit a cigarette, stuck it in a wooden holder, and asked, 'I don't think they'll fire me just yet, will they?'

She shrugged her shoulders. 'Where do you get such ideas?'

He smiled sadly. 'You're laughing,' he said, 'but it's not funny at all. They're quick these days to fire older men, and it isn't easy to find a job. Recently I had to deal with one such elderly man who had been embezzling money for several years, trying to put something away for his old age. Somehow he managed to get away with it, and was declared irresponsible. There are many such cases.'

He stopped talking and stared at his hands. Suddenly he looked into her face. 'Agnieszka,' he said, and she sensed alarm in his words, 'do I look my fifty-five years?'

He moved his face closer to hers, and she felt his unhealthy, sour breath. He looked far older; he was creased, bald, his skin was flecked with liver spots, and there were heavy bags under his eyes. He was ruined, what is called ruined, by the war, by discomfort, by poor food: his muscular body, strong as an animal's, contrasted with his aged face. She gazed at him for a time – he reminded her of a poor old dog; she could think of no other comparison. She averted her eyes, and burst out laughing.

'You look forty-five at the most,' she said. 'I think that, generally speaking, you have nothing to worry about. Many men would envy you your strength.'

He breathed with relief. 'You should practice gymnastics,' he said. 'It helps a great deal.' Then, suddenly changing his tone he asked, 'Where is Grzegorz?'

'I don't know,' she said. 'I've just got in. Has no one come to see Grzegorz?'

'No. Do you have any idea where he might be?'

The mother, who had remained silent until then, spoke. 'Why ask her? She doesn't care about what goes on at home. She has to run around with her boyfriend, that's the most important thing to her. You could die, I could die, but she must let herself go with him.'

'Do you want me to let myself go with you?' Agnieszka asked.

The mother sat up; for a moment they stared at each other. Then the mother closed her eyes, and her face took on her usual martyred expression. Agnieszka banged the door and walked out to the kitchen. Without turning the light on she put the teakettle on the gas range. Only now, lifting the heavy kettle of water, did she feel a pain in her hand; she held it up to her eyes, and examined it in the light of the street lamp – her knuckles were bruised. She gazed at the hissing blue flame, thinking, 'Tomorrow you won't come. Tomorrow the key will be under the mat, as you have agreed with Roman, and no one will pick it up. If there were a thought-reading machine, you'd know what is happening to me. I doubt if I can ever tell you myself. People can't understand each other in these matters. In what matters can people understand each other? When it comes to borrowing ten zlotys, a pair of shoes, or a wringer. That's the limit of our possibilities. Someone said once that darkness separates man from man; we once heard it said, both of us. And here's a gas flame. It gives a bit of light, a bit of warmth. We can make tea. Or cook oatmeal for breakfast. But we can do more. We can throw out this kettle, lock the door, snuff out the flame, and try not to think of anything. Not to think that father is gradually turning into an ape, that in a moment I must go back in to them and go to bed and that we surely won't meet tomorrow . . .'

Her father came in. 'Mother wants her camomile tea,' he said. He walked over to the lightswitch and put out his hand.

'Don't turn on the light,' Agnieszka said. Her face was still wet.

He stopped. 'Are you dreaming?'

'Yes.'

He sat down; as usual he clasped his hands on his knees. He bent forward to her from the waist. 'I'd like to know what about,' he said, trying to sound jolly.

'A fairy tale prince.'

'Has he got a palace?'

'Not at present, but for several years he lived in a palace.'

'Was it built of crystal?'

'Yes. And concrete and steel.'

'What did he see from his window?'

'That depends. I suppose not much. They put iron shutters of some kind over the windows, to discourage you from running away. There was probably a humanistic intention behind it, but if anyone sings you a song about a prisoner who gazes at the blue sky from behind his bars, you have the right not to believe it. In fact, nothing can be seen.'

'What are you talking about, Agnieszka?'

'It's all right,' she said. 'Everything is all right. You look forty-five, and next year we'll increase production of

47

tyres for tractors by fifteen per cent. In the end Zawadzki will move out of here, and our sky is not empty: a few weeks ago there were pictures of Polish jets in all the newspapers. We'll also export Polish motor cars to Pakistan, and the number of miners who are amateur beekeepers will increase fourfold. Everything is all right,' she cried, 'only don't ask me to tell you what I think about and how I think!'

He rose and came over to her. 'Mother has irritated you,' he said in a low voice. He put his hand on her shoulder. 'You must be indulgent towards her. Remember, she has been bedridden for several months, and no hospital wants to admit her. You know that the hospitals are overcrowded. You must be indulgent.'

'Mother is incurably ill,' said Agnieszka. 'The doctors know it better than you. They won't admit her because they have to save others. She will die here.'

He loosened his grip and sat down heavily. She saw that he was staring at her face, and she drew back further into the darkness.

'In the end they'll admit her,' he said after a while.

'No,' said Agnieszka. 'We must have no illusions. Under the circumstances, while there is no room for others, they shouldn't admit her. She must stay with us.'

'Don't you love Mother?'

She shrugged her shoulders. 'Her fate concerns me,' she said.

He passed his hand over his forehead. He had suddenly begun to stoop, and was now merely a pitiful old man, his strong muscles notwithstanding.

'I often think about it,' he said. 'This would probably be best for her. Why should she suffer unnecessarily in this house, with me, with you, with those drunks in the street? The end is always the end. We must understand that moment, when everything is behind us. Old age is creeping up on me, too. There should be houses where old men could be done away with painlessly. When I am no good for anything, I'll ask Grzegorz to give me some sleeping pills. Maybe his chemistry will come in useful, after all.'

'Then why worry?' Agnieszka said. 'You'll meet Mother in heaven, and there you'll continue your wonderful life together. And now, enough of this nonsense. Turn on the light, we'll make the camomile tea.'

There was singing in the street. She closed the window with a bang. She walked over to the stove, and staring at a lid of a saucepan, she thought, 'Where are you going now? What are you feeling, what are you thinking? How can one find one's way in this tangle of drunkenness, concrete, insane ravings, and foolishness? If I could only know what you look like just now. Will we meet tomorrow? And if we do, what will we say to each other to begin with? "I'm sorry" – no. "I was carried away" – no. "I don't know why I acted like that" – no. Do you know what? Let's agree not to say anything. We'll never say a word on this subject. We'll go straight for the key; we'll open the door and we'll find ourselves at last within four walls, no one will be there, no bad memories, and everything, everything will be possible . . .'

'It's boiling,' her mother called from the living-room. 'Can't you hear it boiling?'

Agnieszka started, her father too. They exchanged smiles.

'I'll go out for a while,' she said. 'I've got a headache.'

'Go and see Zawadzki,' her father said. 'He'll be pleased.'

'Is he tinkering with his motorcycle?'

'Yes.'

She smiled again. 'Don't worry,' she said. 'Everything will be all right. On Sunday you'll go fishing. That's always something.'

He sighed. 'Two more days,' he said. 'I must wait.'

'That's nothing. You'll feel better then.'

She threw her coat on again, and ran down the stairs. In a corner of the courtyard Zawadzki had built a garage for himself out of rubble, where he kept his motorcycle. She found him bent over the engine.

'Good evening,' she said. 'Two more horses and you'll be able to go.'

'Maybe you should go to bed,' he said without raising his head. 'Young women shouldn't wander about at night. Might give them foolish ideas.'

'Why? I feel like talking to you. How's your fiancée?'

She squatted beside him. He ground his teeth. 'If she thinks she's fooling me,' he said, 'she'll have an unpleasant surprise.'

'Better men than you have been deceived by women,' Agnieszka said.

He suddenly stood up. He lifted the electric bulb attached to a long cable and let the light fall on his face. 'Agnieszka,' he said dully, 'take a good look at me, and tell me whether I look like a man who can be treated like a moron.'

Lit up from below, broad-shouldered and tall, with sharp features, he looked formidable. 'I've seen you somewhere before,' Agnieszka thought suddenly. 'No, not you. Someone who looked the way you look at this moment. Exactly like you. He even raised his left hand the same way. Where was it and who was it?'

'No,' she said, 'you don't.'

'If all they say is true,' he said, 'I'll beat her up like the boys in the army beat up a whore who gives them a disease.'

'What disease has she given you?'

'I'm afraid that after that it would be hard for me to believe in people,' he said. 'I have seen a great deal in my life, but I don't want the first woman who comes along to make a complete fool of me.' He raised his grease-smeared face to her. 'I want to believe in people,' he said. 'In the end, that is the most important thing of all. God damn it, can't you understand?'

'Has no girl ever deceived you?'

He laughed unpleasantly. 'Nor will any. By God the Father! I was in a concentration camp and I was at the front; sometimes I thought I was in the very centre of hell. After all, that teaches you something, don't you think?'

'Of course,' she said. She looked at his face again. 'Where have I seen such a face,' she wondered. 'What was it? A man desperately stretching upward – that tense face expressing extraordinary concentration. Where was it? When?' 'Devil take you,' she said to Zawadzki. 'I once saw someone who resembled you terribly. I can't remember when or where. Now I won't sleep all night. Good night, Zawadzki.'

She went back into the house. In the hall she ran into her father. He had his overcoat on and was taking his hat from the peg.

'Are you sure Grzegorz didn't say where he was going?' he asked.

'No, he didn't,' she said. 'All he said was that he wouldn't drink any more.'

'Mother can't get to sleep,' he said. 'She's worried about him. I must find him.'

'Go to bed,' said Agnieszka. 'Why get shouted at if you oversleep tomorrow and are late for the office? I'll look for him myself.'

Once again she went downstairs, thinking, 'And you, where are you? Did you go out and get drunk, like Grzegorz? And now you're raving; you are buttonholing people, and telling them our story which concerns no one but you and me. Is that what you're doing? Or are you lying somewhere with your eyes open and repeating my name, Agnieszka, Agnieszka? Perhaps you're afraid of tomorrow, like me? If at this moment you can understand and guess something, remember: I am with you now. I am with you even if you are lying in the gutter. Even if you've lost your mind and gone to some whore. I am with you everywhere, if only you will think of me.'

In the doorway she ran into Zawadzki: he was taking his motorcycle out.

'I'll ride a bit to try it out,' he said. 'Where are you going?'

'To look for Grzegorz.'

'He's drinking?'

'I don't suppose he's down on his knees in some church.'

They were now in the street. Zawadzki kicked the starter, and the engine began to throb. 'Get on,' he said. 'I'll give you a lift downtown.'

They started noisily. After about a hundred yards, the engine began to cough. The motorcycle gave a few violent jolts, and stopped dead. Agnieszka jumped down from the saddle.

'It's the fuel line again,' Zawadzki said.

He looked utterly dejected. They stood in the light of a street lamp, and the glow coming from above illumined his sharp features, now immobile. Agnieszka started. 'Now I know,' she said.

'What?'

'Where I saw a face like yours. Perhaps not a face, but a man standing in the same pose as you now, with the same expression.'

'Well?'

'It was in a film once. A terrorist accidentally kills a man; he must escape, though he is wounded. The whole city is chasing him – the police, stool-pigeons, assorted rats; everyone wants to catch him, each group for its own reason. Also his girl is looking for him.'

'That's noble of her. And . . .?'

'In the end she finds him,' Agnieszka said. She smiled. 'She finds him when he is already dying, and he has no strength left to run. The police are closing in; I remember the searchlights of the police coming closer and closer. The girl decides to die with him. I can even remember the last words of the film. The dying man asks, "Still a long way to go?" And she answers, "It's a long way, but we'll walk it together."'

She stopped.

'And what then?'

'They die together, Zawadzki. They're killed by a burst of police bullets. But that isn't the important thing. They believed to the end – that apparently it was necessary, that it was worth while, and not otherwise. Life always holds the threat of separation, but death joins for ever.'

'You're stupid, do you hear?'

'I hear you. Good night.'

She walked away.

7

She looked for him in all the downtown bars, but he was
nowhere to be found. She looked into the ones where the
elite have their fun, and into the ones where officials
bring bottles of vodka in their briefcases and pull the top
off under the table. At the Kameralna, Grzegorz's
favourite doorman, the mighty Miecio, winked at her
and whispered: 'He was here, but he took off into town.
He's been in love lately, correct?' 'Yes,' said Agnieszka.
By now, after inspecting hundreds of drunken faces and
talking to doormen, she was completely exhausted; she
was unsteady on her feet, and could only think, 'Sleep,
sleep . . .' Miecio took her by the hand and led her to the
office; he poured a glass of vodka into her, and said, 'Go
to the Zieleniak. He went there to get drunk.' He put her
into a taxicab and slammed the door.

'You want to go there?' the cabby said, surprised,
when she gave him the address. He whistled. 'It's no
place for young ladies.'

'How do you know, damn it,' Agnieszka said
furiously, 'which places are for young ladies?'

He raised his hand and adjusted his mirror to catch the
reflection of her; every time they passed a street lamp he

55

slowed deliberately and took a long look. He said nothing for a long time; the taxicab, clanking noisily, dragged itself through the silent city. Finally, he burst out laughing. 'You don't look like one,' he said. 'You really don't.' He sighed, then added, 'A man's stupid to the end of his life.' He put his hand on the meter. 'Here you are. Enjoy yourself, you're a big girl now.'

She paid the fare and got out of the cab. She walked among standing carts; the horses were asleep, their heads down, noses stuck into their feed-bags. Not a single star gleamed in the sky; only the needle above the Stalin Palace glowed, dim and bloody. The immense Zieleniak Square was dark and dead, but she knew that at sunrise it would break into a life of feverish bustle, dubious deals, the rustle of crumpled notes, and hastily exchanged whispers. 'Little obscenities are spoken loudly,' she thought, deftly stepping over a drunk, 'Big ones are whispered. As for the truth, one doesn't say it at all. Who can tell whether each truth is not at bottom the greatest obscenity of all?' A horse neighed directly over her head; she jumped aside, swearing aloud.

The place was an enormous barracks; it was much frequented by the lorry-drivers who brought fresh produce into the city. As she came in, she saw him at once. He was sitting near the bar, at a table wet with beer; he was drawing complicated designs with his finger. At the same table a drunk was asleep, his head down. When Agnieszka sat beside him, Grzegorz did not even look up.

'Are you saving mankind?' she said.

'Correct.'

56

'And?'

'The energy of hydrogen bombs. That is the only thing that can fill one with optimism today.'

'Very prettily said. Wouldn't you like to come home?'

'She didn't come?'

'No.'

'Mother hasn't died yet?'

'No.'

'Nothing has changed?'

'No.'

Only now did he raise his eyes towards her. 'Then what are you here for?' he said.

'I want you to come home.'

'You have a sense of humour.'

'You know Mother can't sleep when you're out.'

'I can't sleep ever. What of it?'

'Grzegorz.'

'Well?'

'I've been looking for you half the night.'

'Your search has been crowned with success, so why complain?'

'Grzegorz, I'm terribly tired. I want to sleep. Nothing else, just sleep at last. I don't know how many nights now I've been looking for you. Do it for my sake, come home. Drink yourself into a stupor, but do it quickly, and come home.'

He looked at her. 'You're very pretty,' he said. 'Your eyes are really green. Your face has a martyred expression. The corners of your mouth are very touching – a kind of childlike helplessness mingled with bitterness. Exiles, and convicts, dream of women like you. That

57

boyfriend of yours must be crazy about you, isn't he? Our parents don't like him because he was in prison. That's strange. Whenever I had a girl, our parents liked her. Until the first abortion.'

'Let's go home now, Grzegorz.'

'Listen to me, Agnieszka. It will be better if you go back alone. I want to go my way to the end. I want to see to what extent a man can stupefy himself. You mustn't watch. Go this minute, and leave me here.'

'Do you want to do away with yourself, Grzegorz?'

'Call it what you like. In this case the name doesn't matter. No metaphor hits it off exactly right. I want to stop loving, suffering, waiting, and believing in things that life doesn't confirm. Do I ask much of my family? All I want is that you forget about me. What right have you to appeal to me in the name of our parents, when you don't love them yourself? Those stupid strangers, full of lies – my only link with them is the address on my identity card – why should we love them?'

She scrutinized him. He was ageing; he looked far older than he actually was. Every day the corners of his mouth dropped a little more, the lines around his eyes grew whiter. He might have been handsome were it not for his perpetually swollen face and his glazed, bloodshot eyes, as green as her own. 'You idiot,' she thought. 'If you only knew how truly I love you. Perhaps more than anyone else. If only I could be sure that you actually do stupefy yourself. I wouldn't be sitting here. I know that you say what you really feel. And I, your flesh and blood, your sister, am sitting here, looking at your gloomy face, and I can't do a thing for you; I can't even drag you

58

home. I wish you could realize this minute that I really can't do a thing for you.'

There was a commotion at the counter. The waiter pulled a man out by the collar; in the doorway one of them gave him a blow with his knee. Agnieszka bent over Grzegorz. 'Don't I mean anything to you, either?'

'This is demagogy,' he said. 'The method is completely discredited. Stalin wasn't successful with it; what makes you think you will be?'

'I don't think. I'm just tired.'

'Everybody's tired. There are two things that tie people to each other in Poland – vodka and exhaustion.'

'Grzegorz, you know that in the end things will be better.'

'I'm sure of it. But tell me, how can we forget what was, how we lived, how people were treated? Party members were rehabilitated after they died, who will rehabilitate me while I'm alive?'

'But you haven't done anything wrong.'

'I had no power. I had only fanaticism. Within my sphere of action I was a scoundrel. I did my best. That means something too, you know. I swear it's easier to purge yourself of great errors than of little villainies. I was Party Secretary at school. I expelled students just because they had an aunt in Pernambuco, or because their great-grandfather had been an informer under the Czars. I tried my hardest, believe me. But now I want to know: just where am I? Am I a swine or a hero? But that's really unimportant: any swine can become a hero if the need for it arises. I want to know what I am to go back to life with. And I want to know for sure that I'll have clean hands in the future.'

'You won't learn it here, on the Zieleniak. Moreover, there's still the idea. An idea that is wise and just.'

'That's true. But the weak point of each wise idea is that stupid people try to carry it out.'

'Those are just words,' Agnieszka said. She was so tired she could scarcely keep her eyes open. 'You're looking for excuses to drink. You can always find those.'

'The very fact that I am alive,' said Grzegorz, 'is excuse enough for doing anything. But I want to know: What next? You say it's an excuse. All right. Let me tell you something. Once I ran into an old schoolmate – I hadn't seen him for a few years. We went to a bar and each of us had a couple of drinks. At that time people like him were referred to as "black reactionaries', in the official meaning of the term. We talked; we had a real heart-to-heart talk. There were many things I didn't like even then, and he didn't either. Then we went our separate ways. This fellow is an enemy. The worst kind. He has no gun, but he whispers, spreads confusion. A man of his sort is more dangerous than an armed gang. In one way or another, his trap has to be shut. And three hours later I met him again – in a security police office. He and I entered the building simultaneously, so it has to be said that history didn't approve of either of us. I defended my faith, my cause before the enemy; he defended his freedom. By God, which of us is a scoundrel, and which a man? To this day I don't know.'

He bent towards her. 'Even supposing that she'll come,' he said, 'that she'll come in the end, as the clock ticks off the last minute of Sunday, that she'll leave her husband and her children, and stay with me – what face

60

will I confront her with, what heart? Am I to love her, if I have stopped believing in myself, if I despise myself? Is the world we're living in a place where love can thrive? We don't sleep with women for pleasure any more, but to have something to tell our friends. I don't want my life to be an illusion. I don't want to have to hide my love. And to begin with, I want to know what will become of Poland. What will happen to those who were wronged? To the party? To freedom? I want to know what will happen to those who betrayed my confidence. To those who kept assuring me that I was fighting and winning, when actually I was retreating, acting against the people, losing my faith and my conscience. You can hear your own voice in your throat, but your own life you can perceive only with your conscience. I want to find water to wash my hands in. Does it make sense to talk about love under such circumstances? Everyone has heard that there is such a thing, but – what does it look like? What should it look like? How can we reconcile pure feelings with dirty hands? That's a problem. Not the only one. Today Hamlet with his "To be or not to be" would be just good enough to serve as errand-boy for a small-town party secretary. Life has smashed all preconceived patterns like so many clay pigeons: what are we to create to take their place? To be or not to be. People are exhausted, they are dropping to the ground, what can raise them up again? To be or not to be. Cynicism is coming – and fast – to be the sole morality. To be or not to be. Can anything valuable come out of a world that has to use blackmail to keep from collapsing? To be or not to be. Oh, we've created artificial moons, but man with his true feelings and aspirations must find a safe refuge. To be or . . . Waiter, half a litre, please.'

The waiter snatched up the empty bottle as he passed the table. Light – the windows had filled with dirty light. A drunken party entered noisily. Agnieszka quickly took stock of them: all of them were well dressed and cheerful.

'It's closing time for the night-clubs,' Grzegorz said. He jerked his head towards the new arrivals. 'Architects. They've come here for the last tankful. It's essential to preserve contact with the masses.'

The waiter came up, put the bottle on the table. 'When will you pay?'

'In a couple of days,' Grzegorz said. The waiter walked away. 'Look at them,' Grzegorz said, 'it may make you feel better.'

Agnieszka turned her head. There was a throng at the bar, the mood was that of a joyful morning. A tall greying man with noble features, dressed in a magnificently tailored suit of English cloth, was slapping the shoulder of a youngster who looked like an apprentice thief and talking loudly: 'I'm not a stranger, I was a boy just like you. From Wola. Before the war I used to go to the Roxy. I loved cowboy pictures. They played that kind at Wola. Do you know Stasiek Malinowski from Wola?'

'No,' the other said, wrinkling his low forehead.

The greying man beamed. 'You see, you see. God, those were terrible times. There was hunger, misery. You couldn't even dream of getting a job.' He raised his hand in a magnificent sweeping gesture. 'Waitress!' he said to the girl behind the counter. 'Princess! One round for all. We'll drink to the working class of Wola.' He added in Russian, 'It's on me.' And, turning to the boy, 'My name's Andrzej, and yours?'

'Kazik.'

'Well, good for you.' He handed a glass to the boy. 'Here's to you, Kazik. And to Wola!'

Grzegorz rose from his seat. He poured the entire contents of the bottle into a mug, and walked up to the counter. He bowed to a lady in a low-cut gown. 'May I join in the toast, gentlemen?' he said.

'Make yourself at home, make yourself at home,' several voices said.

'To the working class of Wola,' said Grzegorz. He splashed the vodka into the face of the greying man and jumped back. A knife gleamed in the hand of the boy with the low forehead. Grzegorz drew out a gun. He raised his left hand. 'Quiet,' he said. 'Don't move. I won't fight the peasant way. I'll shoot.'

They walked out. Outside, Agnieszka said, 'Feel better?'

'A little,' he said. He put the gun back in his pocket. She gave him a sideways glance.

'I can't say you lack Polish characteristics.'

He shrugged his shoulders, then smiled weakly. 'He said himself he liked cowboy pictures,' he said. 'We must penetrate into the dreams and aspirations of the working class, understand its strivings . . .' He paused. After a while he asked, 'Will she come on Sunday?'

'I'm sure she will,' Agnieszka said, apathetically. She did not believe in herself, in her own words, or in the fading sky.

8

The large hand of the clock was approaching the figure
twelve. 'It's seven,' Agnieszka thought, 'he won't come.
Surely, he won't come.' She felt relieved, and for a
moment this drowned out her regret. She was standing
under the clock of the Central Station. It was Saturday;
people seized with the weekend madness were rushing
towards the platform. Loaded with parcels and suitcases,
they pushed and cursed each other in the crowd. The
loudspeaker blared hoarsely, announcing departing
trains; red and green lights went on and off just below it.
She looked at the clock again. The hand had passed the
number twelve by three minutes. 'It's all over,' she
thought. 'So this is what it looks like: lights, noises, and
crowds. None of those feelings that others call suffering.
Nothing but stupor.' The hand jumped another minute;
when she lowered her eyes, Piotr was standing in front of
her.

'I couldn't get on a streetcar,' he said. 'It's Saturday,
the big rush. Three times the militia made me get off the
step!'

She smiled. 'Couldn't they sense that you were going
to join me?'

'They don't sense things,' he said, 'they're the militia. Let's get out of here. I don't like railway stations. They always remind me of good-byes.'

They still had not moved from the spot. They stared at each other. Piotr was pale, his eyes were tired. The loudspeakers blared: 'The train for Minsk Mazowiecki leaves from . . .' People rushed by in packs. Agnieszka asked, 'Are you angry with me?'

He shook his head. 'You can get used to anything,' he said. 'Other people did it better than you. They put on thick rubber gloves for the job, the kind miners use. With a glove like that, you can keep punching a man's face for forty-eight hours without leaving a mark. Only the gums swell up a little, like babies" gums when they cut their first teeth. I remember, one night . . .'

'Let's go,' said Agnieszka. 'What time did he say the key would be there?'

'From six o'clock on. It's there now.'

'So what are we waiting for?'

On the way they stopped at a little café. The customers huddled in groups at the round tables, buzzing like flies. A bald fellow sat swaying at an old-fashioned piano made of light-coloured walnut; his eyes closed, he banged out a tune with thick fingers. 'He's taking a nap, the rascal,' Agnieszka thought, and she was surprised to discover that this angered her. After a long while, a stout waitress brought them coffee and cakes; the coffee was almost completely cold, the cakes were repulsive. Piotr was silent; his head down, he was stirring his cup with a spoon unthinkingly.

'You look like a booby,' Agnieszka said furiously. She felt a growing anxiety.

65

'I'm glad of it,' he murmured.

'How about saying something?'

'I'm afraid,' he said. 'I've always been afraid. Nothing's ever come off the way I wanted, and now I'm as scared as hell.'

Under the table Agnieszka kicked his leg. He winced.

'And what about me?' she said, her voice quivering hysterically. 'What am I to say?'

'I suppose you've slept with someone before, haven't you?'

She looked at him with hatred. 'Now I'll sleep with you,' she growled. 'That's the only important thing, isn't it?'

She jumped up suddenly and grabbed him by the hand.

'Let's go.'

'The bill, for heaven's sake.'

'Leave the waitress everything you have, but let's go.'

They walked out in a hurry, the cloakroom attendant staring after them in surprise. The street ran off into darkness, the twilight irradiated by an occasional street lamp as they walked quietly side by side. He wanted to put his arm around her; she pushed him away.

'What's the matter with you?' he cried.

She stopped. She looked intensely at his face. He had to close his eyes. 'Pietrek,' she whispered.

'Yes.'

'What did you feel when you slept with a woman for the first time?'

'I was sort of happy.'

'At being a man at last?'

He laughed drily. 'Not at all,' he said. 'That I'd never be a woman.'

'What are we going there for?'

'We can go back.'

He saw a moment of hesitation on her face.

'No,' she said. 'Let's go. I only wanted to know.'

Again they walked in silence. When they passed by a street lamp their shadows overlapped, and glided past on one side. Cats were screaming on the roofs. Agnieszka smiled unpleasantly. A cold mass of air blew in from the Vistula, but she felt so warm that she opened the top buttons of her blouse.

'This will be the first time since I was in prison,' Piotr said suddenly.

'What?'

'With you.'

'Really?' she said unthinkingly.

'Yes. True freedom doesn't come at once.'

'Still a long way to go?' she asked after a while.

'Near. A few steps. A hundred yards. Fifty yards. Twenty. Here.'

They entered the house. They climbed a staircase. Somewhere higher up an invisible cat was mewing; Agnieszka suddenly longed to murder it. The staircase smelled of laundry, sauerkraut and fried potatoes, and Agnieszka thought suddenly, 'This has happened before. All this happened before somewhere. This staircase, the cat . . .' A man going downstairs glanced at them absent-mindedly; Agnieszka could barely keep from crying out, 'Why are you staring like that, you half-wit!' Then they came to a door; before it was the cat they had heard. It spat at them once and ran away. Piotr bent down and reached under the mat. He felt a long time, then stood up. 'It isn't there,' he stammered. 'He hasn't left it.'

'Knock,' she said sharply.

He hesitated. 'Perhaps he couldn't . . .' he began.

She interrupted him. 'Knock!'

He knocked gently. No one answered. Agnieszka walked up to the door and kicked it with all her strength; the kitten lurking on the stairs mewed desperately. There was the sound of shuffling steps within, then the key creaked. In the doorway stood a young man with a girlish face. He wore green pyjamas; his breath reeked of alcohol.

'Ah, it's you,' he stammered at the sight of Piotr. 'Damn, how absent-minded I am! The fact is I completely forgot. I'm terribly sorry. Well, never mind, we'll manage somehow. Please, come in.'

He stretched out his hand into the dark corridor. He swayed on his legs a little, but it was clear that he was trying to keep sober. Piotr said, 'No, thanks.'

'Go in,' said Agnieszka. She pushed his back with all her strength. They walked into a long old-fashioned corridor, stumbling against trunks and cupboards. There was a smell of mothballs, and a strange odour of old paper and lavender. The young man in pyjamas walked ahead of them, clever in the way he kept steady on his feet.

'Here,' he said.

They entered the room. Only a little bulb was glowing. The first thing Agnieszka saw was a completely naked girl sleeping on the bed. When they came in, she did not open her eyes, she did not even start. 'Drunk,' Agnieszka thought. The young man explained with an embarrassed smile, 'I met her on a train. She was going to visit somebody, her husband or fiancé, or whoever.' He spread his hands and winked at Agnieszka. 'Well, that's that,' he said. 'It's a small world. In the end everybody meets in bed. But there's another bed. You can do your business, just strip off the cover. We won't disturb each other.'

'Thanks, it's very kind of you,' Agnieszka said. 'We'll do our business in the privy some other time. Is it your kitten mewing on the landing?'

'The kitten?' the owner of the flat repeated. 'The cat? Yes, it's mine.'

Agnieszka turned to Piotr. 'Punch him in the jaw. Quick!'

Piotr walked up to the owner of the flat and struck him with his fist in the temple. The young man dropped like a log.

'That's for letting an animal starve,' Agnieszka said.

'Let's go,' said Piotr.

'Just a minute.'

She walked to the switch and turned it on. The room grew very bright. Agnieszka squatted near the girl and began to examine her.

'Have you lost your mind?' Piotr hissed. He tugged her hand. 'Let's go!'

'I must take a good look at her,' she said softly. 'Come here. See? She has a pretty mouth, nose . . . it's a pity she's drunk, for we might have seen her eyes. Brown?

69

Blue? Black? It would be interesting to know who is waiting for her. See the nice breasts she has? She can't be more than twenty, I tell you.'

'You've gone mad,' he said.

'No,' she said. She covered the sleeping girl and eased a pillow under her head. 'But I'd like to go mad. That would be best.'

She rose and walked over to the window. He saw that she was trying to control her tears. He did not go near her. She put her hand on the flowerpot; he saw her white fingers.

The owner of the flat came to. He got up, his eyes were dazed.

'What's this . . .?' he stammered.

Agnieszka turned round. 'Punch him in the jaw, Pietrek,' she said quickly.

Piotr swung out. The young man fell again, upsetting a chair.

'That's because you don't water the flowers,' Agnieszka said, and smiled at him. 'You don't treat either flora or fauna properly. Good night. No hard feelings.'

In the street she burst out laughing. He gripped her arm. 'What are you doing?' he growled.

They stopped.

'You can't say anything about this situation,' she said. 'Surely nothing like this happened to you in prison.'

He drew back. 'It's better we should split up,' he said. 'I'm telling you, Agnieszka, it's better we should part. In every human relationship there is a line one mustn't cross. It's better to give up and save one's memories at least. Respect. Dignity. Despite everything, these things aren't as silly as they may seem.'

She smiled again. 'So that's all life has taught you? To give up? That prison you're always talking about?'

'Yes,' he said. 'It's better to give up than to watch everything sink in the mud. I have no desire to die. I must live with something. I must remember something. Something that isn't crap.'

'I love you,' she said. 'And I'll stay with you. I want to go to bed with you today. I don't care where or how.'

A party of revellers passed them; they took up the whole width of the pavement, reeling gaily. Piotr and Agnieszka moved aside. Piotr said, 'Come to my place.'

'Your place? But you live with four friends.'

'Perhaps they haven't come back yet,' he said with despair. 'It's Saturday, it's early, perhaps they've gone somewhere. We'll lock ourselves in and won't open the door for them even if they throw me out tomorrow.' He shouted for the whole street to hear, 'Come for a moment! At least for a moment!'

They turned back. Again they walked side by side. Silent, they listened to the echo of their own footsteps. They passed bars, shops, cinemas. Agnieszka looked into lighted windows and thought: 'Walls. Four walls. Perhaps three? Can there be a room with only three walls? Could one live in such a room? Is there such a room somewhere?' She tried to think of different things, but one thought dominated all the others – she wanted to sleep, to fall asleep at last. She did not recognize the streets along which Piotr was leading her. She came back to herself only when he had led her through a doorway and they found themselves in a completely dark courtyard. She looked about her in surprise: not a single window was lit.

'Why is it so dark here?' she asked.

'Don't you see?' He laughed. 'These are ruins.'

Only now did she notice that the windows were empty. She had not been able to see it at first; the windows barely stood out against the dark sky.

'Is this where you live?'

'We're the only tenants,' he said. 'We've fixed this place up ourselves. We climb up to our room by a ladder. It's better than a circus. But that's unimportant. They're not in. Do you understand? We're alone, Agnieszka.'

'Alone,' she repeated. She suddenly put her arms around him, and drew him to her; she began rapturously to kiss his eyes and mouth. 'Alone, alone,' she stammered. 'You understand, you understand?' She pressed herself to him with all her strength. At that very moment a rectangle of light fell on them from above. She closed her eyes. Piotr pushed her away gently.

'They're back,' he said. 'Only one window is ever lit here. Mine.'

They raised their heads and looked upward. High above them, over the window, the courtyard and the ruins, stars gleamed through the mist. Some animal ran by them, its soft paws thudding on the pavement.

'Tomorrow is Sunday,' Agnieszka said hoarsely. 'We'll go out of town, do you hear me? We'll take a blanket and go out of town. To the woods, anywhere. Come for me tomorrow, before noon.'

She wrenched herself free and ran away; she did not want him to see the tears running down her face. She ran like a madwoman, pushing the passers-by aside. Only after noticing that people were turning to look at her did she stop running, and began to walk very slowly.

She stood before her house; she had no courage to enter. 'Not there again,' she thought, 'not there again.' When she finally made up her mind to go upstairs, she met Zawadzki in the doorway: he was taking out his motorcycle.

'I cleaned the carburettor,' he said proudly. 'Now it should work. Want to take a ride with me?'

'Thank you very much,' she said. 'I don't carry life insurance.'

'You make up for it by being disagreeable,' he said. 'If you're interested, your little brother is drinking in the bar three houses away. I saw him there a moment ago. Go and get him before he goes any further.'

He turned over the engine and drove off. 'Go for him?' she thought with despair. 'Or leave him alone, let him do what he wants?' Suddenly she heard a monstrous crash, and turned round. At the corner of the street Zawadzki had run into a man pushing his cart out of the market. The whole street was littered with apples. Zawadzki and the vendor were abusing each other so loudly that the whole street seemed to quake.

'That's a fine thing, too,' she thought.

She entered the bar. At one time it had been owned by a gigantic sailor who weighed more than thirty stone; now he was gone, and only caricatures that had been drawn of him remained – pictures on the wall of a colossus holding a cruiser in his hand.

Agnieszka walked up to Grzegorz. 'Grzegorz,' she said, 'this time I haven't been looking for you. You can believe me, it's an accident.'

'I believe you,' he said. 'Sit down.'

'Grzegorz,' she said. 'For the first time in my life I beg you to have pity on me: go back home. I've been without sleep for so many nights that I can scarcely stand on my feet. Mother won't fall asleep, she'll have hysterics again, and I'll have to look for you again.'

'She didn't come,' he said.

'No,' said Agnieszka. She was silent for a while, then she said, 'Grzegorz, you have a gun. Kill me, kill Mother, kill anyone you want, but come back home.'

'One more day,' he said. 'If she doesn't come tomorrow, it will mean that there's no sense waiting for her any longer.'

They fell silent. Then she noticed that he was saying something to her. She looked at his moving lips, but no longer understood anything. Her head was drooping, all her thoughts were confusedly woven into one – she thought of sleep. She pulled herself up suddenly. 'Grzegorz,' she said, 'drink to my health. To my love. To Sunday.'

She filled his glass. When he raised it to his mouth, she grabbed his hand with her two hands and pressed it with all her strength. The glass cracked; Agnieszka squeezed her fingers ever more tightly and felt the fragments of glass sinking into his flesh. He did not cry out; he only turned pale, and thick drops of sweat appeared on his forehead. Both watched his blood dripping on the dirty tablecloth. She squeezed her hands together so violently that her collarbone made a cracking sound.

'Come,' she said.

He rose; still holding his hand and without relaxing her grip, she led him through the room and out into the street. Only there did she let go of his hand. She staggered heavily and leaned against a wall. 'Hit me,' she whispered.

He smiled. 'That was very nicely done,' he said. 'I thought people had been entirely sterilized, incapable of such imagination. Man's strength always flows from cruelty. That is the basis. It's a pity you've revealed yourself so late; I might have got suitable work for you before.' He walked up to her, and raised her face. 'Come, little one,' he said. 'Yes, let's go home. I'm beginning to like you for the first time.'

9

When she woke, her father was already shuffling about the room in his slippers. She was still full of sleep, she was coming from very far away, when she heard a noise, and that noise – monotonous, steady – chased the remnants of sleep from her eyelids. She lay motionless, as though self-enclosed, not having the courage to open her eyes and make sure. She opened them only when she heard her father walk over to the window.

He drew the curtain and stood there, stooped over, helpless. His hand resting on the sill, he looked out into the street.

'It's raining,' he said after a while. He drummed with his fingers on the glass. 'Low-lying clouds,' he said. 'It will rain all day.'

Agnieszka threw on her robe and walked to the window. She stood beside her father. The roof glistened, water gurgled in the gutters; pedestrians were walking fast, hitching their clothes up above the wet street.

'Snow,' said Agnieszka. She touched the pane. 'Rain with snow. Such things can happen even in May. It was sultry all week.'

'But why Sunday of all days?' her father asked despairingly. 'Why must it rain on Sunday?'

'A Communist trick. To discourage people from going to church.'

She dressed hurriedly and went to the kitchen. Zawadzki was shaving, whistling off-key.

'Good morning,' she said. 'Where's Grzegorz?'

'He's gone out some place.'

'Are you going?'

'Where?'

'To Julia.'

'Her name isn't Julia, it's Maria,' he said angrily. 'Where did you hear that?'

'No matter. Are you going?'

'In this weather? Are you out of your mind?'

'What of it? You cleaned your carburettor . . .'

'I'll go next Sunday,' he said. 'Don't worry, I'll fix her. There hasn't been a woman yet who could make a fool of me.' He suddenly turned to her. 'Why the hell are you so interested in all that?'

'You've cut yourself,' said Agnieszka. 'You should be careful when you shave. And I'm not a bit interested. I'm just being sociable.'

Grzegorz entered the kitchen. He threw off his wet coat, sat on his bed and began to pull off his shoes.

'Are you sick?' asked Agnieszka.

'Why?'

'You're going to bed.'

He raised his bloodshot eyes to her. Then he pointed to the window. 'Find me something better to do.'

'You might go and have a drink now,' she said. 'You'd be drunk by evening and could go to sleep without complications.'

Zawadzki walked out saying, 'Have your fun without me.'

Agnieszka sat on the bed next to Grzegorz. 'Why don't you go now,' she said. 'It's all the same to you, isn't it? If you get drunk now, there's a chance you'll be run over by a streetcar or a truck. Then we'll have some peace. At night the city is empty.'

'I never begin to drink before six in the afternoon,' he said. 'The world is going bankrupt. A man must keep his morale.'

'Grzegorz,' Agnieszka said, 'I want to take advantage of his exceptional moment of sobriety. If you don't stop guzzling as of today, I'll go to the secretary of your party cell and tell him what you do. You shouldn't be in the party. They certainly don't need people like you.'

He looked at her attentively. 'You're too late, little sister,' he said. He patted her on the cheek. 'Yesterday they took away my card.' He smiled. 'A wretched nation. Wretched people. They want to accomplish something at any cost, but unfortunately everything has been done before. The most you can do with my secretary is go to bed with him. Between two meetings. Is there anything else you want to tell me?'

Agnieszka was silent. She stared at the window-pane washed by the rain. The other side of the street could not be seen at all.

'Grzegorz,' she said after a while, 'how much of a swine can one be?'

'I'm interested in that question, too,' he replied. 'I have devoted myself to it entirely. When I reach my final conclusions, I'll let you know.'

'Does she know about it?'

'What she?'

'That woman of yours.'

'As far as I know I have no woman.'

'You're waiting for her.'

'I've waited for other things, too. Nothing came of them.' He rose suddenly. 'What do you want of me? If you're looking for answers to current problems, read the *Banner of Youth*. They once conducted a discussion as to what a Young Communist's love should be like. Very instructive. The little stinkers had more to say on the subject of women than Balzac. And now let me sleep.'

Their father came in. 'Mother feels terrible,' he said. 'She has pains around her heart, she says. I've no idea what to do.'

'It's best to do nothing at all,' said Grzegorz. 'Then at least your conscience won't trouble you for taking part in anything. Couldn't you discuss these world-shaking affairs out in the hall?'

Agnieszka drank her tea and went downstairs. Piotr was waiting for her in the doorway.

'Let's have a cup of coffee somewhere,' she said. She raised the hood of her coat. 'Let's not discuss that subject today. That will be best.'

He nodded.

The café was crowded: they could not get a table. They took a streetcar that was heading downtown. On the front platform some drunks were fooling around; they must have had their liquor that morning, for all of them were wearing their Sunday best.

'Do you know what?' said Piotr. 'Have you ever thought about what Poland looks like?'

'What do you mean?'

'The image of France is Marianne,' said Piotr. 'The Americans would like the Statue of Liberty to be the symbol of their democracy. Russia was at one time represented as a bear. And what is the symbol of Poland?'

'I don't know.'

'I've often thought about it,' he said. 'Do you know what I think it should be?' He pointed to the drunks. 'A fellow like that one over there, in a cheap tennis outfit. Slightly drunk. In some enormous waiting-room. Without a timetable. To make the picture complete, he might be holding a copy of *King Spirit* in his left hand. A bottle in his right, for balance. Is my idea very stupid?'

'I don't know. Maybe it's stupid, maybe it's intelligent. It's raining, that's the important thing.'

The downtown cafés were crowded, too. They walked from one to another, drenched and chilled. They tried to go to a cinema, but despite the rain there were long queues of people in front of them all, standing with newspapers and briefcases over their heads. At the State theatre, a placard announced that the performance was sold out.

'We can go somewhere to get dinner,' said Agnieszka.

'I'm sorry, but I have no money. And you?'

'I haven't either. I spent all my allowance looking for Grzegorz.'

'We can always go to church,' said Piotr. 'It's free, and there's room enough. People still love to pray. I think those various details are related. More seriously than the Lord God Himself might wish.'

'Where shall we go, Pietrek?' she asked dully.

'I don't know. There's no place on earth for lovers.'

They stood facing each other at some point in the wet city. They were both dripping wet. Wind-driven waves of rain kept coming down. They were spattered by passing cars, pushed by pedestrians. A woman's voice was blaring from large loudspeakers.

'Don't talk like that,' she said with despair.

'I read somewhere that man's greatest unconscious wish is to become a slave,' Piotr said. 'I am beginning to believe it. I catch myself wanting to return to prison. Not to think, not to worry about anything. Life isn't worth living, if there is a "Keep out" sign before every place on earth. The only thing I want is to be sentenced. The article of the code and the term don't matter to me.'

He grabbed at her hands. 'I'll go back there, do you hear? I'll do something that will make them put me in prison for years. I'll go back there and be done with it. We won't have to wander about any more, no one will chase us away . . .'

'Come,' she said.

She took him by the hand, and almost by force dragged him after her. They walked into some ruins. She began to run without letting go of his hand; they stumbled over bricks and holes in the ground, got up again and ran on. In the end she dropped onto the ground littered with tin cans, shards of broken bottles, and sodden clay. She pulled him after her; he fell on top of her. With all her strength she grabbed his head by the hair, and pressed it to her breast. With her right hand she began to pull down his trousers. 'Let's be done with it, do you hear?' she cried into his ear. 'Please, don't change your mind. It doesn't matter, I tell you. People aren't any better than animals. We mustn't think we can be different. We can't do a thing about it. Don't think about what'll happen next. Come, now, please! Come, don't run away!'

'Get away,' he cried, 'get away, or I'll kill you!'

'Kill me,' she said. 'Kill me, but afterwards. Afterwards, we won't be able to look at each other. And there will be peace. Peace at last. Without longing. Without love. Without Sunday. Without talk about your prison. Of course, we'll be disgusted. So what? All that isn't important. Don't run, I won't let you. Come. Later we'll forget about each other. And there will be nothing. Now, come.'

He wrenched himself free, and jumped back. Some bricks slipped, and cascaded down with a roar. For a moment he stood over her, his face dark, his hand raised to strike her. 'Agnieszka,' he stammered hoarsely, 'Agnieszka.' Then he ran down the little slope, bricks and rubble tumbling after him. She lay motionless and the water poured over her hair, her face, and her bare hips. A little while later, when she was in the street again, Piotr was gone. A small group of people had taken shelter from the rain in a doorway, and every now and then they stuck their heads out, staring up at the leaden sky. A boy kept repeating, 'Damn it, damn it!' 'It's all because of those bombs,' someone was saying. 'All because of those bombs. If they didn't explode them, the weather would be different.' The whole world was full of water; one had the impression that everything was dissolving.

At home, her father stood by the window, just as he had that morning. Grzegorz was asleep in the kitchen. Agnieszka took her coat off, and sat on the couch. Her mother lay with her eyes closed.

'No fishing,' said the father. 'How could I go out in this rain? My God! I borrowed fifty zlotys from Lipinski for tackle, and all for nothing.'

Suddenly she saw his face close to her own, distorted with fury. She drew back violently, for it looked as though he were going to grab her by the throat.

'Without you,' he said in a breaking voice, 'without that drunk in the kitchen, I could have lived like a human being. Today, Sunday, I could have gone to see a whore, or got drunk. One day of rain, and a man's life is ruined. I must stay at home and nurse your mother. I didn't go fishing, and tomorrow I'll have to shove my way into a streetcar.'

Suddenly he jumped to the couch on which her mother was lying.

'Get out of that bed, you bitch,' he shrieked. 'Get up, die, do anything, but let it be different, let something change at last, let something change . . .'

Agnieszka was once again in the street. A boy in his teens asked her, 'May I offer you my umbrella?' The dark clouds lay low, just above the roofs.

10

'Where did you meet Elzbieta?' the man asked.

'We studied together,' said Agnieszka. 'We even graduated together. Then after two years she stopped studying. I hadn't seen her since.'

'And you met again only today?' he asked. He offered Agnieszka his cigarette case; she was already somewhat high, and couldn't manage to take out a cigarette. The man smiled. He extracted one and stuck it into her mouth. His hands were strong, tanned, his wrists covered with thick hair.

'Today,' said Agnieszka. 'I was in a doorway waiting for the rain to stop. She happened to be there, too, somehow. Touching, isn't it? There was once a hit song called "Stormy Weather', do you remember?'

He shook his head. His hair was dark, short-clipped, without sheen. A lock fell over his forehead.

'No,' he said after a moment. 'Please sing it. Perhaps I'll recall.'

'Here? In this dive?'

He moved closer to her. She felt his breath on her neck – hot, saturated with tobacco and alcohol.

'We can go somewhere else,' he said.

'What you mean is – to another dive.'

'I didn't say that.'

'Too bad. Besides, it's raining.'

'I'll try to cast a spell on the sky.'

'It's a pity I didn't meet you before.'

'Why?'

'I'd have asked you to do it this morning.'

'And now?'

'Now, it's all the same.'

'To you, maybe.'

'Don't you think our conversation is pretty damn stupid?'

He smiled broadly, but his eyes did not change their expression. He looked at her calmly and coldly; Agnieszka could barely endure his stare.

'Don't be too hard on us,' he said. 'Most people talk the way we're talking.'

'And the rest?'

'I don't know. Perhaps even more stupidly.'

'Yes,' said Agnieszka. 'Too bad I didn't know that sooner. Who is Elzbieta dancing with?'

'Some idiot.'

'I think it's a friend of yours.'

'Rather a close one – my own brother.'

He beckoned to the barman, who came up to them like one in a trance.

Agnieszka stared as the glasses filled up with a dark liquid. She bent forward a little and saw the distorted reflection of her own face in them. She drew her head back sharply.

'Let's drink,' said the man.

She picked up her glass; it was very cold, covered with moisture.

'To whose health?'

'To the rain,' said the man. 'If it hadn't been for the rain you wouldn't have met Elzbieta. If it hadn't been for the rain Elzbieta wouldn't have brought you here. If it hadn't been for the rain I wouldn't have met you. Why don't you want to drink?'

'I'm drinking,' she said. She raised her glass higher. 'To the rain.'

They drank. Once again the barman flashed by with the bottle. More and more people thronged around them.

'Where are you going in the summer?'

'I don't know whether I'll be able to go anywhere at all. I have to write a master's thesis. I get my degree this year.'

'Master?'

'Philosophy. A profession that consists in infallably explaining the phenomena of life. Comical, isn't it? And what are you?'

'A newspaperman. A profession that consists in writing the whole truth, the honest truth. Comical, isn't it? Of the three of us, if I'm not mistaken, Elzbieta is the best off. Just a whore. A profession without miracles or illusions.'

'That's not a profession,' Agnieszka said. She smiled. 'That's a morality. An obvious whore – that's the highest moral status a woman can attain today.'

He looked at her sideways.

'What you say has a certain freshness about it,' he said. 'Usually the story is different: "When I was a young girl I

86

met a man and I fell in love with him and he . . ." and so on.'

'Bah,' said Agnieszka, 'that's just talk. The ideal is life without illusions, without myths.'

'You don't want illusions?'

'No.'

'What *do* you want?'

'To forget,' she said. 'My God, if it were possible to forget. Forget my father, these joints, the part of town I live in . . .'

He put his hand on her arm and drew her to him. She closed her eyes and submitted passively.

'Forget,' he said softly. 'Forget . . . for one day.'

11

'Idiot,' said the man; he was purple with rage. He pulled her head up by the hair and slapped her face twice; for a moment she felt the taste of salt. 'Couldn't you find someone else for your first time? The amount of money I spent on our drinks would have got me a decent whore. Dumb cows. Even in something like this you can't be trusted.'

He got into his pyjamas and jumped out of bed. He pulled the blanket off her.

'This looks great,' he said. 'Exactly as if I'd murdered somebody. I'll look great, too. My wife will come back from Stalinogrod in three hours. Damn it, we've no spare sheets. What will I tell her?' He took a deep breath. 'What on earth got into you? You're so good-looking, you should be an experienced whore. What have you been waiting for?'

'For the rain and for you.'

'I'm sorry I flew off the handle,' he said. 'Excuse me, I apologize. You must help me somehow. There's hot water in the bathroom . . . Do you think these can be laundered?'

'Easily,' she said. 'Worse things than that can be laundered. Turn off the light, I'll get dressed.'

'I don't want to see,' he said furiously. He lit a cigarette and turned away. 'If only they dry in time. That cow will come in and make scenes all night long. I'd like to get some sleep, I have so much to do tomorrow . . .' He turned to her violently. 'And what the devil have you been waiting for? Didn't you have some boyfriend? I simply can't get it through my head!'

'I told you: I've been waiting for you.'

'Now you're going to make a scene because I seduced you, I suppose. Dammit, what's your name, anyhow?'

She burst out laughing. 'No scenes,' she said. She walked up to him and kissed him. 'I'm very grateful to you.'

'What's your name? What should I call you?'

'Anything you want. "Darling" would be best. The word means nothing and can be made to fit anyone. Perhaps you say it to your cat. Treasure. Sweetheart. Whore. Whorelet. Little Sun. That's good, too, isn't it? Little Sun will be best. We met during the rain, so it's because we've longed for sunshine. Everything man does, he does out of longing for a better life. Or out of a sense of moral protest. Yes. That's best – Little Sun. Help me take off that pillowcase, it'll be quicker.'

'Listen,' he said. 'Now I'm really sorry. I'm obtuse, forgive me. We must see each other, somehow. I simply can't get it through my head.'

'It's nothing. Don't be upset.'

'How shall we meet?'

'We won't meet at all. We'll think of each other. That'll be enough.'

She washed the bedlinen for him, and then she held out her hand. 'Good-bye,' she said. 'My name's Agnieszka. Agnieszka Walicka. Tell your friends about me, if you want to. And now give me twenty zlotys.'

'What!'

'Twenty zlotys. For a taxi. Yes, yes. Everything must be done properly.'

He drew out his wallet. 'Perhaps you need more.'

She shook her head. 'That'll do, to begin with. Good night. My regards to your wife.'

It was still raining. She could not find a taxi anywhere; she walked through empty streets. Only an occasional window was lit. 'What time can it be?' she wondered. 'Twelve? One? Two?' She had a headache. She walked with her hands in the pockets of her raincoat and her wet hair fell over her forehead. She knelt beside a puddle, and washed her hands in it. Then she rose; it took a moment before hundreds of lamps stopped whirling and settled back in their proper places. She smiled. 'It's over,' she thought, 'now it's all over. It didn't even hurt as much as they say. The only thing I can't understand is why my nose bled. Welcome, life. Tomorrow it will surely be raining, but in a few days the weather will clear. Men will go around without coats. I'll wear a light dress, go to an ice-cream parlour or to the banks of the Vistula, or leave town. Now it's filthy. Even the shadows are sticky.'

She walked a long time before she reached home. A man came out of the doorway and stood before her. It was Piotr. He held out his hand. A metal object gleamed in the dim light of the street lamp.

'A key,' he said in a low voice. 'We've still four hours till daybreak.'

She leaned against the wall. 'Have you been waiting long?' she asked.

'All night,' he said. 'But I knew you'd come.'

'What time is it now?'

He looked at his watch. 'Three.'

'What key is that?'

'I found an apartment,' he said. 'Don't ask how – by a miracle. The owner is going abroad, we can stay there some time.'

'Why don't you sleep?'

'No,' he said. 'I've waited too long. I said to myself that the first night there I must spend with you. Let's go now.'

'At seven it will be day,' she said. 'Maybe earlier. Maybe at six.' She gripped his arm. 'Listen, I want to tell you something. It may be unpleasant, but it's better than a lie. There's someone else. I've been with him a long time. I love him. Once we quarrelled – it was then that I met you . . . You must forgive me. If it relieves you, you can slap me in the face. I want to go back to the other man.' She suddenly pushed back his hand. 'Take the key and go away.'

She followed him with her eyes as he walked away. The mist and the rain muffled his steps; it seemed to her that she longed to hear them with her heart, but she heard nothing. He walked alone down the empty street – tall and slender, his head down. The street lamps drew out his shadow, and it seemed to her that he himself was a shadow gliding along the damp wilderness. He continued to hold out his hand, like a blind man; when he passed a street lamp, the key flashed. She stuck her fingers deep into her throat and bit them to keep herself from crying; her mouth was full of blood. She leaned against the wall, for the world had begun to swing dizzily. He vanished round a corner, but a moment later he re-emerged and walked towards her. She stared at him wide-eyed, but when he came close she saw that it was Grzegorz.

'What are you doing here?' he stammered. His knees were bending under him, he had to hold on to the entrance door.

'She came?' said Agnieszka.

'And went.'

'Why?'

'People told her that I'd been drinking, that I drank. I said that I would keep on drinking. She returned to her husband, to bestow her pure caresses on him. With her slightly worn virtue. Now I have nothing to wait for. I can drink without illusions.'

He paused.

'Nevertheless you're crying.'

'But I love her,' he said. 'I'll always love her.'

Once again he fell silent.

'Grzegorz,' Agnieszka said suddenly. 'Do you have your gun?'

'Why?'

'Do you have it?'

'I have.'

'Come with me,' she said.

'Where?'

'Close by, Grzegorz. This time, really close by. Come, but first give me that gun.'

92

He handed it to her. She slipped the heavy metal piece into her pocket. 'Let's go,' she said.

He followed her. They walked a few dozen yards, turned left, and found themselves in the empty market. They walked around boxes and piles of rotting vegetables. Somewhere a dog was barking.

'Sit down,' said Agnieszka. She pushed a box under him, sat next to him, and put her arm around him. 'Grzegorz,' she said softly, as one speaks to a little child, 'you have talked to me for so many nights, now listen to me. Things in this country won't improve very soon. All of us have waited for a day that hasn't come yet. And won't come soon. It won't come in a week, in a month, or in a year. We have to wait. We must have strength. And most of all, we must live intelligently, far more intelligently than before. We must not let ourselves be deceived, we must struggle, defend ourselves against swinishness. Perhaps things will be all right later. Do you have the strength to wait, Grzegorz?'

He was silent. 'Perhaps she'll come back,' he said finally.

She smiled. 'So what?' she said. 'The novel you told me about once is a stupid fairytale for schoolchildren. And that woman? She'll come back or she won't come back. And suppose she does? People will throw mud at you and pull you apart again. You'll never get a chance to tell each other what binds you together and what stands between you. You'll think continually about her, about her husband, about what is going on between them at that moment . . .'

'That's enough,' he said.

For a while they said nothing.

'You see,' Agnieszka said after a while. She drew out the gun. For a moment she struggled with the slide, then a cartridge snapped into the chamber. 'But you won't live to see all that,' she said. 'And when all of us are living better lives, you will be nothing. A drunken rag, a beggar who believes in nothing and in whom no one believes. Your time is up. You will be like a dead man among us . . .'

'Finish your speech,' he said. 'Poland was killed by speeches.'

'I've finished,' she said. 'And, beginning tomorrow, I want to sleep. I want Mother to die in peace. Take this gun, the safety catch is off. Now I'll leave, and you'll do it. You won't wait for her any longer and be tormented by defeat. You won't enrol anywhere, you won't have to believe in anyone. No one will deceive you. Neither the government, nor a woman. Everything will be snuffed out. Take it.'

She handed him the gun. He took it listlessly.

'One more thing,' she said. 'You know that I love you. Kiss me.'

He bent towards her and kissed her on the cheek; his mouth was cold and hard. She shook her head.

'Not that way,' she said gently. 'Kiss me as if I'd never been your sister . . . Wait, I'll kiss you.'

She kissed him. 'Grzesio,' she said, 'don't think that everything is ending. Think that everything is only beginning. Everything that life should be – peace, freedom and silence.'

She walked a few steps and then ran across the market. Later, in the street, she stopped. He joined her after a few minutes.

'You knew that I wouldn't do it,' he said.

She shrugged her shoulders. 'Of course,' she said. 'I only wanted to show you that all of us are comical with our little stories. Just comical . . .' She began to laugh. 'Now you don't exist any more,' she said, 'nor does Pietrek. There is only the other one, with his wife from Stalinogrod. What does she look like? What does someone deceived look like? What do we all look like? There was nothing. Neither you, nor Sunday, nor anyone. There was nothing at all. To think that way is best. And now there is only freedom. That damn, shitty freedom.'

She began to laugh, and kept on laughing. Later, in bed, as she listened to the breathing of her father and mother, she was still laughing. And it seemed to her that this room, this city, this world, everything was filled with laughter, which no one could hear except herself. Then it was dawn.

12

She was dressing; classes began at eight. She was about to enter the kitchen when Zawadzki came out of it. His face was solemn; he put a finger to his lips.

'Quiet,' he said. 'She's still asleep.'

'Who's she?'

'Maria, my fiancée, well . . .'

'She arrived?'

'Didn't your parents tell you?'

'No,' she said. 'I came home very late last night.'

He looked into her tired eyes and smiled jeeringly. 'Yesterday,' he said. 'Last night.' He smiled happily. 'Those things people were saying were all lies. Life would be easier if there weren't so many kind souls around. Quiet, I think she's just got up. Grzegorz and I slept here in the hall.'

They went into the kitchen. A girl sat with her back to them, combing her hair.

'Marysia,' said Zawadzki, 'this is Agnieszka, whom I told you about.'

The girl turned around, and Agnieszka started. She was the same girl she had found with Pietrek in the flat of the young man in pyjamas. 'Then you looked even more innocent,' Agnieszka thought. 'And your eyes are of a bronze colour, just as I thought.'

'Good morning,' Agnieszka said. 'I see we're in the same boat.'

Maria raised her eyebrows in surprise. 'But we don't even know each other,' she said.

'Never mind,' said Agnieszka. 'We will, and we'll help each other somehow.'

'We're getting married this week,' said Zawadzki. His face was radiant. 'I'm going to attend to the formalities. I've had enough of separation. Congratulate us.'

'I congratulate both of you,' she said. 'And you particularly. You've been so worried. Now, you see! Virtue is always rewarded. After all, that's what keeps the world going. Good-bye. I must go to my classes.'

Zawadzki and Maria smiled at her. She nodded. She went back to her room to get her bag. Her father stood by the window, looking out into the street.

'Low clouds,' he said. 'Now it will pour all week.' He turned to her. 'My God,' he said, 'my God, I wish it were Sunday.'

KILLING
THE SECOND DOG

For Jul Godlewski

Introduction

In the period following Joseph Stalin's death in 1953, Marek Hlasko was unquestionably the most acclaimed and popular contemporary writer in Poland. Relentlessly, he depicted the oppressive bleakness of life there ten years after the war. His rise was meteoric, and it is still extraordinary to recall how brightly his star shone, and how briefly.

Hlasko was born in 1934 in Warsaw, '. . . the city of my youth which . . . will always be without a smile,' he would bitterly recall in a letter to his official critics in 1958, '. . . along whose streets wander the drunkards and the miserable; . . . in which a cheated man unthinkingly goes to his death.' Forced to work from an early age, he had little formal education and left school completely at sixteen to take up a series of jobs as a taxi driver, lumberjack, bargeman, and truck driver over the next four years. At first hand he knew the violent, seamy life at the bottom of society, which would shape him as a writer and would figure centrally in his fiction. Clearly, this was also a time of self-education when Hlasko must have read avidly, for his early fiction bears clear traces of a wide range of literary influences.

At just twenty years old, the young writer literally burst on the scene in 1954 with an excerpt from a novel written earlier. Then, as editor of the student weekly *Po prostu*, which he turned into a major national paper, and as a prolific, widely published short-story writer and book and film reviewer, he simply dominated Polish literary life in the middle 1950s. In the book of his collected stories entitled *A First Step in the Clouds*, brought out in two editions during the explosive year of 1956, and some months later, in November, in his stunning first novel, *The Eighth Day of the Week*, Hlasko gave voice to the rebellious longings and bitter disenchantment of the younger generation. Polish and Western critics alike were lavish in their praise and generous in forgiving any faults in this brilliant but raw new talent. In the West he was likened favourably to the writers of the Beat Generation and to England's 'angry young men', and many of the stories were translated and anthologized; three were made into films. *The Eighth Day of the Week* was brought out in fifteen languages, and in less than two years a film version was completed and presented at the 1958 Cannes Film Festival. More honours followed when Hlasko was named the most popular contemporary writer among young Poles and was awarded the prestigious State Publishers' Literary Prize for *A First Step in the Clouds* in 1957. He was a star and an idol, but he was also a kind of rebel hero for his insistence on the primacy of human feelings and of independent thought.

On the surface everything seemed to be going in Hlasko's favour, especially when he received an official visa to visit the West for two months in 1958. Yet one could detect, mixed with the critical praise in the Polish press, jarring, ominous warnings about the 'lack of ideology and collectiveness' and about the 'threat of nihilism'. More disquieting was the refusal of the Polish censors to pass for publication two new short novels, *The Graveyard* and *Next Stop – Paradise*, notwithstanding the fact that the latter had already been made into a film in Poland. In France, the author, frustrated and angry, gave the novels to the influential Polish émigré journal, *Kultura*, for publication. From the official point of view, it was bad enough that *The Graveyard* was a cutting, satirical attack on Stalinism in Poland, and, it should also be said, an uncharacteristic political stance for Hlasko. But publishing abroad was considered a crime. Vicious attacks appeared in the Polish press, and permission to extend his visa was denied. In the end Hlasko decided to stay abroad and fired off a courageous, moving letter to his critics, which was also refused publication in Poland. Later, he spoke of returning home 'in the near or more distant future', but more than a decade of exile and restless travel followed. He never would return.

In his early works, with the notable exception of *The Graveyard*, Hlasko did not attack the established order or the official Socialist Realist orthodoxy; rather, he disregarded them completely, as if they did not exist. Ideologically indifferent, interested in human experience and feelings, not politics, he made his main theme the unequal struggle of the young for real love against cynicism and random joyless cruelty. There is something moving in his lyrical assertion of love as the only hope,

105

defence, and even liberation from the hellish world of dangerous and violent night streets, strewn with filth and the drunken bodies of broken people. But it is a losing struggle. Agnieszka, the heroine of *The Eighth Day of the Week*, cannot find a place for love, even alone with her Pietrek, and she gives herself to the first man she meets with the words, 'The ideal is life without illusions.' Her brother, who has lost his lover, his work, and everything in his life, drowns himself in alcohol, saying, 'I want to stop loving, suffering, waiting, and believing in things that life doesn't confirm.'

Hlasko's dry-eyed, spare style recalls Hemingway, whom he acknowledged as an influence, and his phantasmagoric vision of the grotesque reality of everyday life owes something to Kafka, Gogol, and, possibly, Bruno Schulz. The same sharp tongue and unsparing eye and the unorthodox view of things that won and kept his admirers incurred the enmity of the cultural guardians in the Party and the Catholic church. In reality, he was neither a 'Beat' writer nor an 'angry young man', but a truth-teller in a land where it seemed that integrity and truth had gone into hiding. He brought them back inconveniently and without permission and was made to pay.

The unguarded confession by Hlasko that '. . . whatever doesn't come from Poland or isn't connected with it doesn't interest me at all,' suggests how painful the years of exile after 1958 must have been. One senses in his restless journeying a vain search for a place, a home somewhere else. After France he travelled to Italy, Switzerland, and West Germany, then settled in Israel in

1959 for two years, working illegally as a truck driver, a manual labourer, and a pimp, if we are to believe his literary biography (*Piekni, dwudziestoletni*) published in 1966. There he met again Sonja Ziemann, who had played the leading role in the film of *The Eighth Day of the Week*, married her in 1962, and moved to West Germany. The next four years were very productive. Hlasko drew on his experiences in Israel for two stories and four short, brutal novels, published between 1964 and 1966. The present work, *Killing the Second Dog*, is the first of these novels to come out in English. He also wrote the autobiography mentioned earlier and a novel set in Poland during the Stalinist time, which appeared in print in 1967.

Things seemed to have fallen apart by 1966 and, after separating from his wife, the writer set out for the United States. Once again, he repeated the now familiar pattern of work taken on illegally for lack of the necessary papers. A novel based on his life in America and published posthumously appears to be the only writing from the almost three years in the States.

In 1969 Hlasko resolved to move back to Israel. He died on the way, in Wiesbaden, West Germany, on 14 June 1969, from an overdose of sleeping pills. He was thirty-five.

Fortunately, it sometimes happens in history that a writer's time comes round again, that in a different age a new audience is found. So, justly, it may be that time for Marek Hlasko. The extraordinary changes in Eastern Europe, especially in Poland, in the last few years have evoked a serious interest in the West in the cultural life in

107

Poland since the Second World War. It is appropriate and timely that we now have in the publication of *Killing the Second Dog* a welcome addition to the body of works by Hlasko available to the newly aware and interested English-speaking reader. The author is fortunate in this fine, talented translation by Tomasz Mirkowicz, which catches superbly the quick, racy dialogue and the 1940s *film noir* mood of the novel. It is no coincidence that two of Hlasko's novels (*The Eighth Day of the Week* and *Next Stop – Paradise*) and three stories were made into films. There is an unmistakable cinematographic quality to his writing, not only in the dialogue and mood, but in the pacing, the visual shape of the scenes, and in the cutting from scene to scene. It is not at all hard to 'read' *Killing the Second Dog* as a film, and that may account for its distinctive appeal to a contemporary reader.

Overall, one can hope that the appearance of *Killing the Second Dog* heralds the future translation and publication in English of Hlasko's other works.

Thompson Bradley
Professor, Russian Languages and Literature
Department of Modern Languages and Literature
Swarthmore College
Swarthmore, Pennsylvania, USA

The ride from Haifa lasted over two hours. About halfway to Tel Aviv, we realized that the man sharing the rundown cab was in a bad way. The driver said we would soon reach the outskirts of the city and put his foot down, taking each turn with a screech of tyres that made us feel like actors in some B-film. At one point a policeman raised his hand to stop us, but the driver didn't slow down. In the rear-view mirror we saw the cop turn to his Harley standing in the shade, but he just shook his head; it was too hot to bother. He stood in the middle of the road, took off his helmet, and started wiping the sweat off his forehead.

'How is he?' the driver asked, without turning around.

'Almost gone,' Robert said and then looked at me. 'Now he'll have lots of quiet and plenty of shade. Think he'll like it?'

'Do you know him?' the driver asked.

I had to hold our dog by the collar; he was fidgeting and growling. The dying man must have made him nervous.

'No,' I said.

In Tel Aviv the stranger died as soon as the three of us carried him out of the cab. He was lying stretched out on a bench while we waited for an ambulance. Some decent soul placed a photo magazine over his face. It had the picture of an actor on the cover; his blue eyes watched us with a piercing stare. Robert lifted the magazine and peered at the dead man's face.

'I think he was Rumanian,' he said. 'Just arrived from Europe. He didn't speak a word of Hebrew.'

'He won't have to learn it now.'

'This is a bad sign.'

'You mean him?'

'What else?' Robert said. 'I'm superstitious. This may spoil the whole deal for us. We should've taken the train.'

'Poor fellow, he's not buried yet, and already he's made another enemy.'

'That's right,' Robert said. 'I hope they stick the bastard in a coffin and bury him deep.' He looked at the driver, who was leaning over the corpse, trying to recognize the actor on the magazine cover. 'We're leaving, chief. Haven't got much time.'

'It's John Wayne,' the driver said finally, lifting his head. 'Can't you wait a bit longer? You know how it is with the cops. They always think everything happened different than you tell them. You'd be doing me a real favour.'

'We have some business to see to,' I said, 'but we'll be staying at a hotel across the street. Fifty-six Allenby. If the cops ask about us, give them our address.'

'Oh, they'll ask for sure,' the driver said, again leaning over the corpse. 'No, I guess it wasn't John Wayne I saw in *Pursued*. Must've been some other guy.'

We crossed the street and walked into our hotel. The desk clerk was sitting at the end of the lobby, reading a book. I thought of the dead man and glanced at the cover that showed some guy murdering some bird, or maybe it was the other way round.

'Had a nice trip?' the desk clerk asked.

'It lasted over two hours,' I said. 'And some fellow we didn't know who was riding with us died right there in the cab. He was leaning against Robert the whole time.'

'Stupid bastard,' Robert said. 'And a bad sign if I ever saw one. Have you got two beds for us, Harry?'

The desk clerk didn't answer. He kept on reading. I glanced again at the lurid cover.

'For ready cash,' Robert added.

The desk clerk finally put the book down. 'How long do you want to stay?'

'We don't know yet,' I said. 'We came here to make some cash. That's why Robert's angry. He's convinced the corpse might mess things up.'

'Are you going to try to marry him off again?' the desk clerk asked Robert.

'Of course. It's worked before, hasn't it?'

The desk clerk looked at me closely. 'He's old. And he looks goddamn tired.'

'Don't worry about me, Harry,' I said. 'Leave it to Robert. He knows how to make those birds part with their money.'

'Sure I know,' Robert said. 'The main thing is to have an idea. And I've still got lots of ideas for this character.'

'He is *old*,' the desk clerk insisted.

'Leave it to me. I know best. That gloomy face is still worth its weight in gold. So, have you got those two beds or haven't you?'

'You'll have to pay for the dog, too. Hotel rules.'

'We've already paid once. When we bought it.'

'How much?'

'Almost a hundred pounds. It's a pedigree. Did you think we got it free? And with a nanny to take it out for walks? You didn't think that, did you?'

'You'll have to pay in advance,' the desk clerk said. 'Four pounds. And I don't want to see that dog running around the hotel.'

'The dog is always with us,' I said. 'Goes wherever we go. We have no secrets from it.'

The desk clerk looked at me again. I knew he wanted to give me a nasty smile, but it didn't come off. His face barely twitched. The day was too hot.

'Some day you'll overdose and that'll be the end of you,' he said to me. 'You barely made it last time. They had to give you oxygen. I thought you were a goner.'

'That's because I hadn't eaten a decent supper. Anyone can make a mistake, Harry.'

'But you already made one in Jerusalem,' he said. 'They had to lock you up in a psychiatric ward afterwards. Room fourteen.'

I went over to the board and got our key. 'I collected a packet that time in Jerusalem.'

'You are old.' He picked up his book and turned around to put our money away. He placed the bills in a desk drawer which he left half-open, too lazy to shut it properly. 'What time will you be back?'

'Before midnight,' I said. 'We'll just take a quick shower now and be off.'

'Have you got your own towels?' Harry asked.

'No,' I said.

'Two towels . . . that'll be half a pound extra.'

'Half a pound won't break us,' I said.

Harry pulled two towels from the drawer. I took them, but Robert grabbed one and gave it back.

'One is enough,' he said.

'Frankly, I'd prefer to have my own towel,' I said.

'You'll have to learn how to save on little things,' Robert said. 'Otherwise you'll never get rich. I read the other day that Chancellor Adenauer demanded to be paid for a TV interview, took the money from the reporter, and pocketed it right there, right there while eight million Germans watched. You should learn from him.'

We walked down the dark hallway. A hunchback was sitting at the far end, reading a book. I made out his face in the slanting rays of a dim lightbulb. It had that fake sweet and painful look that cripples often have. I glanced at the book he was reading, *The Life of St Paul of Tarsus*.

'A fellow Catholic,' I said. 'Though not for any idealistic reason, I assume. And a hunchback at that.'

'I converted to Catholicism because the priests promised to help me get a Canadian visa,' the hunchback explained. 'What's new? You still alive?'

'Don't worry about me,' I said. 'And you, I see, are still sitting in front of the bog. Nothing's changed, has it?'

'Well, I feel safer here,' he said, pointing at the toilet door. 'If I get the runs, it's only one step away. Anyway, none of your business.'

'I've known this clown for three years now,' I told Robert. 'And all that time he's been sitting in front of the bog. Isn't he something?'

'We could use him,' Robert said.

'How?'

'Oh, I'll come up with something. A hunchback has plenty of potential. But all I can think of now is taking a shower.'

'Hey, blondie,' the hunchback called after me, 'the priests promised to give me some cash at the end of the week. Find me a broad, okay?'

'That'll cost you thirty or forty pounds,' I told him.

'Why? Everybody pays twenty.'

'Yeah, but not everybody is a hunchback.'

'They say I'll get the money when I learn the catechism. I've already memorized the Ten Commandments. Now I'm reading the life of St Paul.' He got up, his face twisted in pain. 'Excuse me, I've gotta rush.'

'What's wrong with him?' Robert asked.

'He couldn't stand the heat. Started drinking fresh water. It was during a khamsin that lasted for eight days. He caught some kind of stomach disease. Doctors are giving him charcoal and other things, but nothing seems to work. Now he wants me to find him a girl.'

'I'm not surprised,' Robert said. 'I bet his whole sex life stops at the wrist. Let's go and shower.'

Shortly afterwards we left the hotel and went into the nearest café. It was a little cooler inside; the rubber blades of an overhead fan quietly cut the air. Watching them you had the illusion of coolness. And after sixteen hours under the scorching sun, even the illusion wasn't something to be sneezed at. Robert ordered two beers, and a waiter quickly brought them to our table.

I looked at our dog. It was lying motionless, its thick paws stretched out to the side.

'He gets on my nerves,' I said.

'Who? The dog?' Robert asked.

'No. Harry. The desk clerk. What does he know? Does he know how much money I made for us last year?'

'Don't give him a thought. Think of your new bride.'

'Maybe he's right,' I said. 'I'm old. It might not work this time, Bobby. If they find me too late, that'll be it.'

'No.'

'You know it could happen.'

'You'll be all right. Just remember to eat more beforehand. Have a big supper first. Besides, your body has built up some immunity by now.'

'Don't count on it. One day it might turn out really shitty. Don't tell me you don't know that.'

'Yes, it could happen,' he said. 'But do you know how stupid I am? I haven't even insured you. And I don't intend to take out a policy naming me as your sole beneficiary. You're not a film star and I won't play your widow.'

'Hold on, I swear I never suspected you of anything like that.'

'Anyway, neither of us is in this for kicks. Hell, I never expected to make my living this way. My speciality, as you know, is Shakespeare. I studied English at university so I could read him in the original. That's exactly what I'd like to be doing now.'

'Let's not talk about that, Bobby.'

'No, I don't mind. Did I ever tell you how I think *Macbeth* should be staged?'

I remained silent. He had told me at least a hundred times – in Jerusalem, in Haifa, during those endless trips together, and during all those nights when it was too hot to fall asleep. It was when he talked about Shakespeare that his ugly face began to light up. Now, I thought, comes the boring part.

'Did I?' he said. Shakespeare was his one true passion and like all cranks he never tired of his favourite subject.

'You did mention it,' I finally said, feeling a little sorry for him. 'You really are a great director, Bob. It's too bad I happen to be your only actor. And I feel pretty worthless now. My face looks awful. I don't think the girl is going to fall for me. Sorry, but I really don't expect it to work this time.'

'It will. It will. Stop worrying. Trust me. I'll make her fall for you. Just remember this, the last time anybody called her a girl was before World War One. And stop thinking about your face. Look, it's like with Shakespeare. Shakespeare's plays shouldn't be performed. You just have to know how to say the lines. The worst thing is that everybody insists on performing Shakespeare; it makes me want to throw up. How can you perform a scene like the one where Hamlet and Ophelia's brother quarrel by the grave? Olivier had this brilliant idea how to perform Shakespeare, so he turned his plays into theatre. Shakespeare is life, not theatre.'

'Don't tell that to too many people.'

'I'm telling it to you,' he said. 'You just have to shout out your lines and walk off the stage. You don't have to

116

perform at all. Anyway, we'll rehearse your part from the beginning.'

'Tonight?'

'No. Tonight we need to rest. But first we have to talk to this backer of ours. Finish your beer and we'll go. It's cooler now.' He fell silent for a moment and then asked, 'What did that fellow say?'

'What fellow?'

'The one in the cab. Did you understand his last words?'

'Not quite. I think it was "pray for my soul" or something like that.'

'He said it in German?'

'Yes.'

'What a cliché,' Robert said. 'But I suppose a lot of people have repeated that hackneyed phrase. Still, it's worth remembering. You can always add a word or two and change something round. I've heard all those famous last words are a pack of lies. When Goethe was on his deathbed, they couldn't get a word out of him for posterity, so they started shining a light on his face until he finally said that famous line of his: "More light!" Sly bastards.'

'I wouldn't say a thing. I'd be too scared.'

'Not even a word to the children kneeling round your bed? Or to your wife banging her head against the floor in desperation?'

'Come on,' I said. 'I'm tired. Let's talk to our backer and get it over with. I want to climb into bed and sleep until morning. Look at the dog. He's beat too.'

Robert paid the bill and we walked slowly towards the sea. It was already dark. I remembered reading in some book that man is but the shadow of a dream, but I couldn't think of the book's title or the name of the author. I don't know who had dropped that line on me or at what point in his life the author had written it. Was it while he was gazing at the dying flame of a candle, or watching a dog with a bone in its jaws, its eyes shining with fearful ecstasy? Or maybe it was the voice of God that had suddenly rumbled inside him and made him mutter those words while staring wide-eyed at the people around him, certain all of a sudden that he would not disappear without a trace when he reached the end of his road. And maybe it seemed to the people around him they had been allowed to glimpse some wonderful light that would never shine again. It must have been a glorious moment and I can only thank God I wasn't present, since most likely I would have added a few words and spoiled the whole show. That's the way I am. And then what would have happened to the light? But I don't like light. I like the darkness, which frees us from our faces and the shadows we cast.

'Is anything wrong?' Robert asked.

'No. I was just trying to remember something.'

'And . . .?'

'No luck. But don't worry. That's why I'm so fond of thinking; it doesn't lead to anything. You should know me, Robert. We've been working together for over a year.'

'Relax, man. Soon we'll start talking about money and you'll feel even worse.'

'You'll do the talking.'

'Right. And you just try not to have such a damn sad face. All you need to do is sit with us; you don't even have to listen to me. You can clean your fingernails or pick up some book and leaf through it. Don't pay any attention to what's happening. To you it should be obvious he'll give us the money. Pretend you can barely hide the boredom and disgust you feel, okay?'

'Okay,' I said.

We were walking side by side. Darkness was all around us, but not the kind that envelops a city like a dream. It didn't make us forget our hot and tired bodies. This darkness was rough and hard, like the dust; and like the dust it clung to our skin.

'So, once again. How will you act?' Robert asked.

'I won't pay any attention to either of you,' I said. 'You won't interest me at all. I'll just sit there looking out at the garden, and your loud, repugnant voices will seem to me both meaningless and unreal.'

'You've got it. Okay, we're here.'

We entered a building and started climbing a stairway overrun by cats. It was siesta; in this country, people sleep by instalments. They go to bed after coming back from work, and then again late at night. They spend their evenings in cafés or visiting friends. When you visit someone, your host usually asks whether you'd like a shower before you sit down for coffee. Robert disliked taking showers and almost always refused, claiming that only dirty people need to wash so often. *Chacun à son goût.*

Our host was sitting on the terrace, reading a newspaper. His girlfriend was sitting next to him. When she saw us, she adjusted herself in her deckchair and lowered her gaze to the floor. It was meant to show her contempt.

119

She was putting on an act. Men look only for peace and deliverance; women have to have something churning and shifting in their lives. They're always very serious about how they feel and genuinely convinced that all those fleeting emotions they take for anger, love, or contempt are going to last for ever.

'It's us, Mr Azderbal,' Robert said.

'Again?' Azderbal said.

'Didn't it work out very well last time?'

'Sure. All it took to save my neck was two top lawyers and a doctor who testified that I happen to be partially insane. I don't suppose you've come here to tell me of some new deal we could make together, huh?'

'That was an accident,' Robert said. 'Somebody squealed on us.'

'Bullshit,' Azderbal said. 'I'm not interested in any more shaky deals.'

I moved away and sat down on a deckchair next to the girl. She glanced at me in a brief, detached way. I could swear she'd been practising that look in front of a mirror for the past three months, certain I was going to show up at any moment. But I hadn't shown up; I had only now come with Robert because we were short of cash. I sat next to her, staring out at the dark garden, while behind our backs the two men continued their loud conversation.

'I need money,' Robert was saying. 'I have to pay for his hotel, food, and all the rest.'

'And for the doctor,' the other added.

'Yes, for the doctor, too. We need money for at least two or three weeks. He must have a room and three meals

120

a day; breakfast, lunch, and dinner. He must be able to afford cigarettes, coffee, a deckchair at the beach, and a haircut and shave once in a while for him to look all right. And our dog, too, our dog costs a pretty penny.'

'What does it eat?'

'Two pounds of pork a day,' Robert said. 'Or do you expect me to cook porridge for it in my hotel room and mix it with canned kosher meat? Do you really? Well, maybe you'd eat that mush, but not this dog.'

'It's too big. You should have bought a smaller dog, a poodle or a Pekinese; this one's not a dog, it's a monster, a fiend. No wonder it's so expensive to feed.'

'Why don't you just say outright that we should use a dead dog? That would work out cheapest. You don't know how to make money because you don't know what investing is all about. You want a hundred per cent profit on every rotten deal you make; you haven't learned that some of the best deals ever made often involve just fractions of one per cent. You think like a small-scale herring merchant who has to make a hundred per cent profit on every sale or else he'll die of hunger.'

'You should have bought a smaller dog,' Azderbal insisted.

'Don't try to teach me, mister. The dog has to be big, happy, and full of life. It must be loved and pampered by everybody. People must want to feed it chocolates, while it knows it can't accept even one piece. Not even sniff it! That's what I call a real dog. A dog like that becomes an issue. And then we have the makings of a tragedy. Don't you see that? The dog must have honey-coloured stars in its eyes.' Robert came up to me and paused behind my

121

chair; he was furious and awe-inspiring. 'I have to tie the wings of my soul while he begrudges me a bit of meat for the dog.'

'He's a fool,' I said quietly, without turning my head. This was how we had planned it; I was to show the backer we despised him and his money, so he would think we had other options and that we came to him only because he lived so close. Azderbal and the girl twitched nervously. I continued to stare into the darkness.

'Why don't you try it yourself?' Robert asked him. 'Then you'll see how difficult it is. You'll see what these women are really like. All those old bitches out to save their lives. He suffers with them and pretends to be their saviour. Two lonely hearts scarred by life and all that stuff. Try doing that yourself! You don't want to? I'd like to see a woman give you forty piastres for a bus ride. Once I've seen that, I can lie down in my grave and die in peace. I'd know I hadn't wasted my life.'

Azderbal looked at me. 'He's too old. He's got the saddest kisser the world has seen since the death of that saint who used to sit on a pillar. What was his name?'

'St Simeon the Stylite,' I said, which was a mistake on my part; I was supposed to remain silent throughout.

'Yeah, that's the one,' Azderbal said. 'What does he do with them in bed? They just cry together, or what?'

'We'll divide the money three ways,' Robert said. 'Like we did last time.'

'How much do you think it'll be?'

'I don't know. Maybe six hundred, maybe eight.'

'He'll never score that much,' Azderbal said, looking at me. 'His face is perfect for playing poker, but not for this kind of game. Either you're blind, Robert, or else you don't want to see this. Maybe you feel pity for him and don't even know it. I can't help you.'

'But he's already made a fair bundle this way,' Robert said.

'He's finished, and you simply can't see that. He's done this trick a few times too many and everybody knows about it. Why don't you find some handsome young fellow and bring him here? Then we might work something out. But don't expect me to stake my money on this one.' He turned to the girl. 'What do you think?'

'He's too old,' she said. 'He's finished. What woman wants a guy who's over thirty and looks ten years older? Women know a man like that's never going to let them change him. And that's all they ever really want.'

This was her way of getting even with me for having walked out on her two years earlier. She'd been waiting for a chance to take her revenge ever since and was probably feeling disappointed that she couldn't do anything more to hurt me.

'Right,' I said. 'Let's go.' I got up from the chair and shook hands with Azderbal and then with her. I added in a friendly voice, 'Maybe we'll make some other deal together, Azderbal.'

'If it's worth my time, you can always count on me,' he said.

'And how do you find her?' I asked, stroking the girl's face. 'Has she learned to fake orgasms yet? She used to be rotten at that. Most likely because she has no sense of rhythm. Most women are deficient in this respect. Good night.'

We left.

'Azderbal is a thief,' Robert said.

'All Azderbals are thieves,' I replied.

'The most thievish family of Azderbals used to live in Wroclaw,' Robert said. 'If they didn't swindle someone at least once a month, they'd be so depressed they'd need a psychiatrist. Some of them even got suicidal.'

I didn't answer. We walked back along the same street in silence. It was only when we were back in our hotel room that Robert finally spoke: 'Don't worry, tomorrow I'll find us another backer. We don't need a lot of money. Just enough for a few days.' He looked at the dog, which was lying stretched out on the floor, its red tongue hanging out. 'But we do need it. There's no way we can cut our expenses any further. No one mourns a Pekinese. Or a pug. Your dog has to capture the minds of all who see it. Otherwise there'll be no tragedy.'

'Have you seen her yet?' I asked.

'I don't need to. They don't differ much from one another.' He moved to the window and stood there, gazing out; I looked at his white body gleaming with sweat, and the sight made me feel queasy. I wished there were a painting or a photograph hanging in the room. Anything you could fix your eyes on. But there was nothing. Only the bare walls, Robert, and the dog. I couldn't look at the dog. 'Yes,' Robert said, 'they really don't differ. All those lonely women getting on in years who want to get married one more time. With their money, which they've been saving all their lives.'

'A man wouldn't do it,' I said. 'You'd never find a man who'd scrimp and save for fifteen years so that he could

124

marry some woman he's never seen, has no idea even what she looks like. Robert, would you put your shirt on?'

'Why?'

'Your body's disgusting. God only knows why I should have to look at it.'

He turned around. 'That's a very good line. An excellent line. You can say it to her at some point. I'll walk off and you say, "I've spent the best years of my life with this guy. At night I'd look at his disgusting body and think to myself that I'd never be with a woman again." And then you take her hand and look into her eyes. Yes, that's a beautiful line. You won't forget it, will you?'

'No.'

'You can even stroke her body when you say it. Though maybe not. Better not overdo things. The dialogue'll be enough.'

The desk clerk came into the room. 'I knew it . . .'

'Anything wrong with knocking?' Robert said, interrupting him.

'The cops are here!' the desk clerk shouted. 'Go down and talk to them. I knew something like this would happen.'

I had to put my trousers on again; they felt rough and hot, covered with dust. I went downstairs, but I didn't feel like walking into the street. I stood in the doorway while the policemen sat in their car and stared at me.

'You again?'

'Good evening, sergeant,' I said. 'Did I do anything to deserve such an unpleasant welcome?'

'Not yet. But you're going to, aren't you?'

'Give me a chance, sergeant. I'm just a sentimental fool.'

'You do it again, we lock you up.'

'There's no law against falling in love.'

'Who's the woman?'

'I don't know. I love her, that's all I know. I love them all, sergeant. My father used to tell me that when he was young he fell in love with every woman he met. I'm his spitting image. Is that so unusual?'

'You got a dog yet?'

'Would you like to see it?'

'Yeah, bring it here.'

I whistled and the dog bounded down the stairs. It settled at my feet. We looked like master and best friend posing for a picture. A perfect pair.

'My God! That's not a dog, that's a horse. Where did you get it?'

'We bought it.'

The sergeant turned to the other policeman. 'Has anyone reported a dog missing? Check it over the radio.'

While the other one switched on his radio, I said to the sergeant, 'Come on, we paid a hundred pounds for this dog.'

'Does it eat a lot?'

'Does it? We feed it tripe . . . and other stuff.'

'You should try canned dog food,' the sergeant said. 'Have you?'

'Yes, but the dog won't eat any. He's as spoiled as a film star. We've had to cut down on our own food to feed it properly. Robert's lost two pounds.'

'The dog's okay,' the second cop said, signing off.

'Let's go then,' the sergeant said. But he kept staring at me. 'I don't want any problems with you two. So be careful. Believe me, one day you and your friend'll go on a long prison diet.'

'You're wrong,' I said. 'And besides, Robert isn't my friend. He's my manager. There's a big difference.'

'Who are you then?'

'His client,' I answered. 'Good night.'

'Good night.'

They left. I turned round and went back to our room. Robert was already asleep. Lying in bed I looked again at his white body. It wasn't a pleasant sight. In a few days I'll be lying in a hospital bed, I thought, and the doctors will be fighting for my life, as the newspapers say. Will my body be as white and sweaty as his? For some reason, it didn't matter to me. I threw the sheet off. It made me feel a bit cooler, but not much. I leaned over, touched the stone floor with my hand, and put the sheet on it. Then I lay motionless, beginning to smell the stink of my own sweat. Finally, I dropped off to sleep.

I woke up some time later. Robert was sitting on the bed, smoking a cigarette.

'I can't sleep,' I said.

'Nor me.'

'Are you worrying about getting the money?'

'No. We'll get it tomorrow. I'm worrying about finding a child. That's why I can't sleep.'

'What do you want a kid for?' I asked. 'Will you want me to feed it my own flesh, like a pelican?'

'We need the kid to show what a kind-hearted man you are,' he said. I could feel his irritation. He was angry that

I hadn't grasped what he had in mind right away. 'She's going to fall for it. Some oaf will start mistreating the kid and you'll be the one to stop him. Every woman has to fall for a trick like that.'

'And you'll be the oaf?'

'Of course. Why waste money hiring somebody else? Don't worry, I can play the part. This is very important. It'll show you in the best light. From that moment it'll be like falling off a log.'

'Can't we manage without the kid?'

'I don't know,' he said. 'It'd be best if she had a kid of her own. With some sort of handicap. A kid with one leg shorter than the other, a hunched back, or at least a stammer. A little hunchback would be perfect. Someone gives him a kick up the arse, and you step in and act like a hero. Yes, a sweet little cripple. Or maybe a paraplegic. Jesus Christ, think how much money we could save that way!'

'Oh, come on,' I said. 'Dreams like that never come true. Besides, who ever brings a hunchback to the beach?'

'Don't you worry. To you it may have a hump the size of a camel's but to its own mother the kid is as straight as the prick of a Russian soldier. What do you know about women? If they're in love, they're as blind as bats.'

I got up and walked over to his bed, which stood close to the window. The street outside was dark, but there was no coolness out there. The night seemed solid and dusty, like some forgotten theatre set. Robert gave me a cigarette, and in the light of a burning match I saw his face was dry and tense. I thought with annoyance that he

128

must have wiped it with our towel that was now lying somewhere on the bed.

'What's bothering you?'

'I'm worried it may not work out,' I said.

'Don't worry. As long as you stick with me, you'll be all right. I'm as durable as the papal state.'

'I know. But one day this con is bound to fail. We'll be the ones to lose money. What'll you do when that happens?'

'We'll come up with some new act.'

'What new act?'

'Any act. We're not any less clever than other men. We have to believe that.'

'Robert, do you know what a loser is? It's a man who keeps on losing. I'm a loser, Robert. You heard what he said: find some handsome young fellow. If you plan to go on with this hustle, one day you'll have to do just that.'

'Hey, that's really good! What you said about being a loser. You have to tell her that. Say you love her, blah, blah, blah, but there's been a lot of misfortune in your life, blah, blah, until a warm female hand grasped yours, blah, blah . . . It'll be great.'

'Robert, art isn't made by people working in twos or threes. Art is made by loners. That's why I used to like literature, because in literature the only ones who count for something are those who go it alone, never expecting anyone to come along one day and explain what they're really striving to achieve.'

'Don't you like literature any more?'

'No, I don't. But it's not that simple. Actually, I never really wanted to write.'

'Don't think about it. Better think about where we can find a kid whose sweet little looks will melt a woman's heart. A kid with eyes like diamonds. Later, we'll give him money for ice cream and he can catch dysentery for all I care. That kid has spoiled my whole night. The fucker isn't even big enough to cut himself a piece of bread and he's already a pain in the neck.'

I lay down next to Robert and he moved over to the wall. We lay like that for a while, listening to the sound of our own breathing. I was sure neither of us would be able to fall asleep, but I didn't care. Looking at Robert, I knew he was thinking about the kid and that his mind was working full steam, coming up with new ideas and rejecting them one after the other. At least I could be certain tonight he wouldn't bore me with his bullshit about the kind of theatre he longed to create.

'You're a loser, too, Robert.'

'Not yet,' he said. 'Right now I'm one of those who've worked out a good angle. It was me who found you and guessed you'd once wanted to be an actor. It set me thinking and I came up with this con. The whole thing is my baby.'

'History will never forget you.'

'What amuses me most,' he said, 'to the point where I wake up at night howling with laughter, is all those women listening to you talk about love and the life you'll lead together. None of them ever knowing all your lines were made up by a fat old Jew suffering from a double hernia who feels sick even after eating wild strawberries with cream. And that I'm that old Jew. You do all the work while I just lie peacefully in bed and wait for the moment when you'll collect the bundle and depart in an unknown direction, whispering the most tender endearments. No, son, I'm not a loser. I'm the one who's created you and this little piece of theatre.'

'Yes, but one day you'll have to come up with something else. I'm sorry, but that's the bloody truth.'

'I'll make you up again from scratch. No problem.'

'I could do with a drink,' I said.

'Everything's closed at this hour. Think of the kid.'

'I hate kids.'

'So do I. All kids except this one. It'll make a nice beginning. You'll both look at the kid, then at each other, and your thoughts will rush up to the Pearly Gates . . .'

'I don't think "rush" is the best word,' I said. 'I think "soar" has a nicer ring to it.'

'Okay.'

'So how should I phrase it?'

'I don't know. Maybe just say, "Let me fly away with you." Don't worry. In dialogue there's no need for perfection. You have to deliver your lines slowly and in a clumsy way, forgetting that you know them by rote. You have to believe these words are your own. And she must see how hard it is for you to speak, how much trouble you have finding the right words and stringing them together. That's the way Shakespeare should be staged.'

'But that's not Shakespeare,' I said. 'It's a line from some song.'

'What is?'

'Let me fly away with you.'

'What's the difference? Just don't forget what you ought to be feeling.'

131

'When am I supposed to say that? After you act out the scene with the kid?'

'Yes. The kid is very important.'

'And then will I . . . you know?'

'Don't worry. I'll tell you when the time is ripe.'

'Let's rehearse some more. We won't be able to sleep anyway.'

'All right.' He got up from the bed and wrapped himself in a sheet. I sat and smoked.

'Where do you want to start?'

'Doesn't matter,' I said. 'Anywhere.'

'All right. Let's start from when she tells you that she's got to go back to the States after her vacation.'

'You first.'

'I didn't want to broach this subject earlier,' Robert said, 'but you know I'll have to leave soon, don't you?'

'My darling, why didn't you tell me that sooner?'

'I'm only a woman . . .' Robert said. 'I wanted to be happy with you for as long as I could.'

'I didn't expect the summer to pass so quickly,' I said.

'I must ask you something.'

'No. Please let's not talk about this. I know what you want to ask. But I can't go with you.'

'Why?'

'I won't bring you luck. I'm a loser, you know. Nothing ever changes for men like me. I'd keep losing just the same on the other side of the ocean.'

'Then let's try to be losers together.'

'You're only a woman. And it's best to be a loser alone. It hurts less.'

'Wrong,' Robert said. 'Your lines should go this way: "You're only a woman so you don't believe in defeat, but

132

I've learned the hard way what it means. It's best to be a loser alone. It hurts less." Will you remember, please? And don't say "It hurts less" immediately after saying "It's best to be a loser alone." Take a pause. You're thinking and struggling with yourself, hating your words, hating yourself for saying them. This is a dialogue, for God's sake, not a litany to Our Lady of Lorraine. These words hurt you. You have to say, "It's best to be a loser alone," then smile like someone who's forced to lend his sports car to his mother-in-law, and only then say "It hurts less." Do you see it now?'

'Yes,' I said. 'Let's move on to the pathetic part, can we?'

'Right. Go ahead.'

'When you're twenty years old, you're unwilling to settle for any compromise where women are concerned,' I said, taking Robert's fat paw in mine. 'Later, you become mature enough to accept compromise. And then one day you learn to love a woman who . . .'

'Louder! You're unable to believe your own words. You feel disgusted with yourself.'

'. . . who is far away and living with another man, but you are happy that she exists, that she's alive and breathing, and you don't care if she belongs to somebody else. You just thank God that she's alive and that you can think about her whenever you like.' I fell silent; I looked at his face, and after a few seconds I looked down and saw the towel Robert had wiped himself with lying on the floor. 'And that is old age, which has come upon you too fast.'

'We will face it together,' Robert prompted.

'One day people stop visiting you and so you start visiting them. That's the onset of old age.'

'A good line,' Robert said. 'Where did you get it from?'

'Some film. I think Fredric March was in it. There was also something about kids. That when you go to visit your kids who've forgotten you, you know you've turned old.'

He put the sheet back on the bed. 'Well, that about wraps it up. You're doing well. Just remember not to speak too fast. Deliver your lines as badly as you can. It has to seem that all the words are your own.'

'Robert?'

'What?'

'Hasn't it ever crossed your mind that these words could be my own?'

'Don't think about that. Try to imagine that I created you from scratch. Disney created Donald Duck, but he probably doesn't believe it himself any more. Same thing with Goofy. Goofy's got his own life now. That's the way you should picture yourself.'

In the morning loud noises woke me up. I pulled on my trousers and walked into the hall. Two men were fighting; one was stretched out on the floor, the other was kicking him in the face with the point of his shoe. The fight was taking place in front of the toilet. The hunchback cowered in a corner, like a gloomy spider. The two men fighting bumped into me; I kicked one, then the other. Their loud cries woke up other hotel guests who poured out into the hall and pulled them apart; both men yelled for the police.

'What was that all about?' I asked the hunchback.

'Me.'

'What did they want from you?'

'They wanted to touch me.'

'Well, then, I suppose you should have let them.'

'It's not that simple. They both make deals in the city. So you see the problem.'

'No, I don't.'

'Both believe touching a hunchback brings luck. But only if you touch him first. That's why they were fighting. They've been fighting over me for two years now.'

'And you?'

'What can I do? When things get out of control, I lock myself in the crapper and wait for the cops. They don't know the truth anyway. My hump is reserved for Azderbal. The old crook comes here every morning before going to the city and he touches me. He pays me ten pounds a month. Though today someone came even earlier and gave me a pound to let him touch first.'

I looked at him. 'That was Robert, wasn't it?'

'Yes. He told me he had to find a new backer. And I let him touch first.'

'And you forgot to tell Azderbal about it, didn't you?'

'It slipped my mind.'

Soon afterwards we went to a small café by the sea, Robert, myself, and a man Robert had found to be our backer. He was a quiet man, not much older than me, but with the build of a professional bouncer.

'Is everything clear?' Robert asked.

'Yes.'

'Right, then give us the money. No point in wasting time.'

'I only said everything is clear.' The bouncer shook his head. 'I didn't say I'd give you the money.'

'You didn't?'

'Look, I need to think it over. And listen, does that goddamn dog of yours . . .'

'I've told you five times already it doesn't bite,' Robert said. 'A strong man like you, how can you be afraid of a dog?'

'The dog may not know if I'm strong or not,' the bouncer said. 'And even if it does, it can still bite me out of spite.' He glanced at the dog. 'Have you had a vet look him over? He's got bloodshot eyes.'

'Give us the money,' Robert said. 'We haven't got time to argue with you.'

'I have to think about it a while.'

'Stop playing games,' I said. 'Our woman is already in the hotel, somebody's making a pass at her this minute. The city's swarming with blokes out to make a quick buck.'

A man came to our table. I could see he'd hit the bottle really hard last night. His face was pale and swollen around the eyes, his hands shaking. He was shabbily dressed and very thin; his frayed shirt, a hand-me-down from someone much taller, hung on him like on a scarecrow. I knew that right now, at nine in the morning, with the sun eating away at his eyes, he was feeling miserable.

'Buy me a beer,' he said. 'Some day I'll stand you one.'

'Go away,' Robert said. 'We're busy.'

'Buy me a beer,' the drunk said again. I could tell by his shrill voice he was unstable: one of those drunks who start crying after the first sip. I took out thirty piastres and handed it to him.

'Here. Go and buy yourself a bottle.'

'I wasn't talking to you,' he said. 'I was talking to him.' He pointed to Robert.

'Take the money and beat it.' I stretched out my hand with the thirty piastres showing, but he slapped it away and the coins fell. 'That wasn't very nice,' I said softly. 'Leave us alone now.'

This made him angry. He poked me in the chest with his finger. 'So you think you're a better man than me.'

'No.' I got up, grabbed him by the elbow, and dragged him to the door. He tried to resist, but he was so weak that I hardly felt anything. The waiters at the door took him off my hands and threw him onto the street. He fell on the pavement, unable to get up. The waiters watched with amusement.

'Don't hit him,' I said.

'This is a place for respectable customers,' one of them said.

'Not while I'm here.' When I got back to our table, I asked the bouncer, 'What's the matter with the waiters? Why do they like to gang up on drunks?'

'You should know,' he said. 'You used to work as one.'

'You know everything about me, don't you?'

'Only what I was able to find out,' the bouncer said. 'I'm the one who's financing this operation. I have to know who's working for me.'

'He's not working for you,' Robert said. 'He's an artist.'

'And how about you? Are you an artist, too?'

'Of course. I've always been one. Nothing can ever change that.'

'Look,' I said to the bouncer, 'if you know so much, then you must know the bloke who wanted us to buy him a beer.'

'I used to.'

'Who is he?'

'We were in the army together,' the bouncer said, 'but then his wife left him and he started drinking. He was married to some foreign woman. Now he's hit bottom. Didn't even recognize me.'

'Another nut,' Robert said.

'In Israel you drive past a nuthouse every two miles,' the bouncer said. He and Robert continued talking, arguing back and forth really. I stopped listening. I was looking at a dark-haired girl in uniform sitting by the window; she reminded me of a girl who had once invited me to her house and whose mother had fainted when she saw me because I looked exactly like some SS man who had killed her uncle and his kids and forced her to watch. The dark-haired girl paid her bill and left. I thought of a man I shared a hotel room with once; he was constructing a bomb he planned to throw at the minister of finance. Since he had no experience at bomb-making, everybody was afraid to stay with him. Then I started thinking of someone else, the brother-in-law of our hotel desk clerk. When his family committed him to a mental hospital, he set the building on fire. All the nuts ran off to some nearby orange grove, dancing and singing, and the police had to search two days for them and move them to other hospitals all over the country.

Robert left the table to make a phone call. He returned right away in the best of spirits, beaming like a turd in paradise.

'Good news!' he said. 'We've got a kid!'

'Where'd you find him?'

'Didn't even have to look. Your new bride's got one of her own. She's a divorcee.' He slapped the bouncer on the arm. 'This is foolproof. The woman is a divorcee. No husband, a child in need of a father, and she's not so young any more. Everything will work out perfect. Give me the money.'

'Okay,' the bouncer agreed suddenly. 'Just write me a receipt.'

'Later. When there's some paper.'

'Write it on a napkin,' the bouncer said. Robert did, but you could tell by the drops of perspiration on his forehead that writing out receipts was not something he enjoyed. The bouncer meanwhile was watching me with the same kind of friendly interest you usually reserve for lizards and spiders.

'Don't look at me like that,' I told him.

'You won't con me, will you?' he asked. He was still staring straight at me, but a helpless look had appeared in his eyes. He seemed surprised by the paper napkin. He held it gently between the thumb and forefinger of his left hand. Robert had given the napkin to him in exchange for the money.

'No,' I said. 'We never con a partner. You can ask anybody who knows us.'

He kept holding the napkin in his hand. He stared at it for a while and then moved his gaze back to me. 'Don't you ever feel sorry for them?'

'Sometimes I do. Sometimes not at all. I felt sorry for one woman. A teacher from Boston.'

'Boston?'

'That's right. Name was Louisa. I got a letter from her later.'

'What did she write?'

'Just one word: "Why?" I never wrote back.'

'You should have. If I were you, I would have written to her.'

'I don't know how to answer letters like that,' I said. 'Put that receipt in your pocket. If you lose it, Robert won't give you a new one. I know him pretty well.'

'Right,' the bouncer said. His thick fingers unbuttoned his shirt pocket and he slipped the napkin inside. His eyes were still fixed on mine and it was getting on my nerves. 'Wouldn't you prefer to lead a different life?' he asked.

'I've never given it any serious thought.'

He continued to stare at me with a confused and helpless look.

'Don't you like my face?' I asked. 'Well, neither do I. Just imagine how nice it would be if I looked exactly like you. Neither of us would need a mirror to shave.'

'Come on,' Robert said. 'Let's get the bullets, then pick up his things.'

'What kind of gun do you have?' the bouncer asked.

'A nine-millimetre pistol.'

'Me too, so you don't need to buy any ammo,' the bouncer said. 'Just don't tell anyone where you got it.'

'Don't worry,' Robert said. 'We've got a gun permit. Come on, let's go and pick up his things.'

140

'Where did you leave them?'

'I never said we had them,' Robert said. 'You're going to lend them to us. A suitcase, a few shirts, and so on. He can't move into the hotel naked and barefoot, can he?'

'You never told me anything about a suitcase and clothes,' the bouncer said.

'I forgot. But I'm telling you now. What's the difference? Anyway, he doesn't need much. Only a couple of things. Is your mother alive?'

'Yes,' the bouncer said.

'How old is she?'

'Over sixty.'

'Have you got a picture of her?'

'I can find one.'

'She'll be his old mother who died a year ago,' Robert explained. 'She had cancer, so he went heavily into debt to send her to a Swiss clinic where she was operated on by a famous surgeon. But it didn't work and she died three weeks after the operation. Her constitution was so weak that she had no chance. Now she's buried in a small green cemetery and he has to pay off his debts. Do you see it now? He needs his passport to leave Israel, but his passport is in the hands of the lawyer who represents the people he owes the money to. All clear?'

'Yes,' the bouncer said. 'But he doesn't look at all like my mother.'

'So what? Hard living has changed his looks completely. Don't worry about things like that. Leave it to us.'

We went to the bouncer's house. He lived in a nice area; the windows looked out over Jaffa. We could see

141

the white needle of a minaret and the twisting streets, and we could smell all the familiar smells: fish, grilled meat, hot copper. While the bouncer was packing clothing into a suitcase, studying each piece separately and folding it carefully like a loving wife, I said to Robert, 'You've got to stay with me, Bobby.'

'Stay with you? Where?'

'At the hotel.'

'Are you going mad? My being there would only embarrass her.'

'No, it wouldn't. Just the opposite. Listen, I've created a role for you: you'll be my best pal, the friend who doesn't want to leave me alone in the middle of my depression. And so on.'

'What do you mean, "and so on"?'

'You know how to work out the rest.'

'I don't like it,' he said.

'Why not? Anyway, I don't give a shit. I don't want to be by myself. I told you I don't believe we'll succeed this time. I just don't. So I need you with me.'

'What about the extra cost?'

'We'll rent the cheapest room. It won't make such a big difference. Anyway the bellboy who finds us all these women should be able to get us lower rates. He makes something on this deal, too, doesn't he? I refuse to be alone, and that's it.'

'Have you lost your self-confidence?'

'I never had any. Remember, it's you who created me. The way Disney created Donald Duck.'

'No I didn't.'

'Have it your way. But if you don't come with me, I'm not going through with it. Do it yourself. You know the script. I'll visit *you* in the hospital. Maybe bring you something to read. If you're still able to read, that is.'

'This is blackmail.'

'You're right. It is.'

The bouncer finished packing my suitcase. Standing in front of us, he took off his shirt and wiped the sweat off his body with it. I watched his rippling muscles. His arm was as thick as a boa constrictor. I burst out laughing, and they both stared at me.

'What are you laughing at?' Robert asked.

'At you, Bobby. Because if this whole deal falls through, it's you who'll have to come here and explain to this joker why he won't be getting his money back. God, won't that be funny!' I got up and moved to the door. 'Bring the suitcase to the hotel. I'm going to get a haircut. See you around, Constrictor!' I added, turning to the bouncer. 'If this whole deal, God forbid, falls through, remember it was his idea, not mine. So don't go chasing after me with that gun of yours. And Bobby, remember to feed the dog. It hasn't eaten yet. I'll be there at two. Try to get us a room looking out at the sea, will you? I'd enjoy that.'

As I was leaving, they started to argue again; the bouncer wanted to give Robert the picture of his mother without the silver frame it was displayed in. Robert insisted the frame was indispensable as additional proof of my filial devotion. He drew a vivid picture of me as a penniless beggar who nonetheless refuses to part with the thin silver frame his mother's picture is set in.

'He could have sold that frame a hundred times,' Robert said, 'when he was hungry or ill. But he didn't! God, you don't understand the simplest things!'

I smoked a cigarette next to a stack of deckchairs guarded by a small boy and watched the woman from a distance. Our rooms were on the same floor, but she didn't know that yet; she had gone down to the beach straight after lunch and was sitting there with a pile of magazines scattered around her, while her kid, a boy of ten at most, was running around like a little devil, making a nuisance of himself. She didn't look too bad; she was one of those women who got a late start in life, and her face was still young and bright. I like women with bright, innocent-looking faces like that, faces that have a nun-like air about them. These are the only faces that provide the emotions and the element of surprise that make life bearable. And that was exactly her appeal. When you wake up in the middle of the night and the cogs of your brain start turning and throttling your heart, and it's almost dawn and you know you won't be able to fall asleep again, you can screen yourself from sadness and anger with the image of a face like that. I could use her face the way a child brings up his hand to shut out the view of something he's afraid of. The boy tending the deckchairs asked me for the third time if I'd like to rent a chair. I did, and strolled down to the beach with it.

I walked right up to her and set my deckchair next to hers.

'This spot vacant?' I asked. I picked up one of her magazines and studied the face of some idiot and then put it back on the sand. 'I'd like to know if this spot is vacant or not,' I repeated.

She looked at me and gestured at the beach, empty except for the two of us. 'The whole beach is vacant,' she said.

144

'I don't care about the whole beach. I'm asking you about this spot.'

'It's not vacant now,' she said. 'Unfortunately.'

'No need to insult me. It's standard practice when people go to dinner, they ask someone to keep their spot for them. A simple courtesy. That's why I asked. If you don't want to be disturbed, put up a sign that says so. Or bring a policeman and make him stand in the sun to protect you.'

'Have you finished?'

'No. Not yet. I'll let you know when that happens.'

I placed my chair on the sand and took out a book and opened the pages at random. I wasn't reading, or, if I was, the text wasn't registering in my mind; I was wondering whether Robert would have been satisfied with my act. I felt he would. He wanted me to be aggressive. Even more than that: to be violent with a fury aimed at everything and everybody. Women didn't trust men who sat down next to them and tried to charm them immediately; all the sweet talk would come later, unexpectedly, at some point when Robert gave me the cue; but first I had to display the bitterness and fury of a poor soul whom the heavens had spared no misery. It was only then that women, each and every one of them, took upon themselves the role of playing go-between in the conflict between Fate and the man they had chosen for their own, the one they would follow through fire and water, to hear the peals of golden trumpets. But nothing could be hurried, the fury couldn't disappear straightaway; it had to dissolve gradually, slowly quieten down, and finally die out like a fire in the tormented soul of someone who's found the ladder to heaven in a woman's gentle touch. That man was myself!

I flipped an unread page and looked over my shoulder. Robert was walking in our direction with a deckchair under his arm, his face twisted from the effort though the chair weighed no more than seven pounds. Poor Robert; he always looked like an insect emerging into light for the first time from under an overturned stone. He was pale beyond belief, and I thought of the bouncer with his brown, dry skin. Robert opened his deckchair and settled into it, breathing heavily through his mouth; then he pulled out a packet of cigarettes and handed it to me. He had scrawled on it: 'An American?' I gave him a light and nodded my head. So did he; this meant that we would speak only English.

'It's a hot day,' Robert said.

'Yes,' I said. 'How clever of you to have noticed.'

'How long have you been here?'

'I went to the consulate and then came straight back. There was a bloody great crowd there.'

'So you did go?'

'Didn't I say I would?'

'If you had asked me for advice . . .' he began.

'But I didn't,' I said, interrupting him.

For a while we smoked in silence. Some old fart and his wife had gone into the sea together and were splashing water at each other like a couple of kids.

'Quite a sight, eh?'

'Somebody should shave that bastard's balls and send him back to kindergarten.'

'For Christ's sake,' Robert said. 'They're just an old couple having some fun.'

146

'No,' I said. 'What they really are are mirrors you can't break. You can never break all the mirrors.'

'I don't like it when you say something you don't really mean,' he said. 'What you said about mirrors was very nasty. It reminds me of someone. He wasn't such a great writer as you might think. And he knew it. Someone who goes hunting for forty-five years doesn't shoot himself accidentally while cleaning a shotgun.'

'Okay, but at least he knew the menus of all the restaurants in the world. And the prices of all the drinks. That counts for something. You probably don't even know how much a Gold Star beer costs if you drink it standing by the bar!'

'Hey, take it easy. I know you've had a hard day.'

'Can I try your patience some more and ask you for a favour?'

'Yep,' he said. He had always liked Gary Cooper and it came as a heavy blow to him when that handsome old fellow died. I remember the day; we went to a cinema on Ben Yehuda Street, and it seemed hard to believe that all the life had gone out of that face brightening up the screen. The whole audience was sad and unusually quiet. I expected any moment someone would come up to me and say: 'It's not true. Some goddamn drunken reporter made it up.'

'What's the favour?' he asked.

'Can you help me brush up on my English, old man?' I said. 'I've landed a job.'

'You've landed a job?' he repeated in a voice full of joy. 'Does this mean you won't have to leave for . . .'

'On the contrary, that's where the job is. I got a letter from my friend in Australia.'

'And . . .?'

'I'm going.'

'Oh, my god!' Robert said.

'Yep. He's found me a job in some local company. And, of course, he's sponsoring me. They've even agreed to pay my fare, something they never do. I've no idea how he managed it. He's probably not only had to vouch for me, but also given them an IOU. I'll have to sign a five-year contract.'

'What kind of job is it?'

'When I was in the consulate today,' I said, 'the officer who has been processing my application . . .'

'I asked you what kind of a job,' Robert broke in.

'In a mine!' I shouted in anger. 'What did you expect? That they'd ask me to lead the Baptist Church in Melbourne, for Christ's sake?'

'No, I didn't. But I don't think a mine is the best place for someone whose field is eighteenth-century literature.' He fell silent; I watched his face in wonder as it slowly turned towards the woman. God, he was absolutely great: the dismay and shock he wanted somebody to witness and his confidence as an actor were truly incredible. Looking straight into her eyes, his face transfixed with horror, he said to me, 'You, a specialist in literature of the Enlightenment, to work in . . .' and then he stopped, unable to go on, as if suddenly he felt totally helpless and everything was unworthy of words.

Now it was my turn to be silent for a while, so that his words would have time to sink in. Finally I glared at him, and, remembering to speak softly, asked, 'Do you think I had any choice?'

He turned to her much more swiftly than you would expect, considering his bulk, and slowly unclenched his fist. In the middle of his sweaty palm lay a crushed booklet of paper matches. You crush matches like that unconsciously, in a spasm of internal anger. 'Do you have . . .?' he mumbled and broke off.

'A light?' she asked.

'Yes.' He took the lighter she gave him and lit a cigarette. But he didn't return the lighter to her at once; he sat squeezing it tightly in his sweaty hand, staring straight ahead as if he'd suddenly gone blind. He was pretending to be utterly shocked by my decision, even though what I had said was the text he had prepared for me.

'Give the lady back her lighter,' I said. The sound of my voice brought him back to life. He returned the lighter, and although I couldn't see his face, I knew it was filled with shame and embarrassment.

'I'm very sorry,' he said.

I glanced at her; her face also reflected embarrassment at having overheard our conversation; and I could see pity in her eyes.

'Don't be,' she said. She smiled, and it was at that moment that something Robert calls the invisible bond of friendship joined their hearts together.

He turned to me with a crazy look on his face, a look that was the natural reaction to the sight of a gentle and sad feminine face.

'Now you want me to teach you English,' he said in a high shrill voice. 'Me, the one who has gone over the whole of Elizabethan literature with you, who has even translated Macbeth's monologue for you.'

149

'That won't be useful to me any more,' I said. 'And please, stop shouting. They aren't going to pay me for knowing Shakespeare, but for pushing wagons of coal. Or whatever else the job demands.'

'What about your future?'

'My future? That's a word I won't be needing any more.'

He jumped up from his chair and stood in front of me. 'Why don't you just kill yourself?' he said, his fat lips quivering. 'Don't you think it would be better for you?'

Hearing this, I also stood up. 'I didn't ask you for advice. When the time comes, I'll know what to do. Just now all I want from you are a few hundred measly words which might come in handy.'

I gave him a violent push and walked away, my back and shoulders shaking with emotion. I dived into the sea and swam around for a while. The water was still warm, but you could feel that in an hour or so the evening cool would come and give the sweltering city a moment's grace. I thought of what Robert was doing now, thought of him just getting up from the sand. I didn't have to turn round: I knew the script.

'I'm very sorry,' Robert says. 'I've never seen him so upset . . .'

'Has something happened?'

He gives her a dead stare. He doesn't understand the question.

'Has something happened?' she asks again, her voice tremulous.

'I thought you heard,' he says.

'Your friend is planning to go away?'

'He isn't planning, he's made up his mind. This is the worst thing that could happen. You know, he belongs to a dying species. He's one of the few who always do what they say. Poor fool, he doesn't even know how unfit he is for surviving in this world.'

'Aren't you exaggerating?' she asks. 'Being a miner isn't the end of the line, you know. One of my cousins . . .'

'He's not one of your cousins!' Robert shouts, interrupting her rudely. He is angry at her for not being able to grasp the simplest facts. 'You don't know what a fool he is. For five years, while studying for his degree, he worked at night as a cab driver to support himself. He studied literature. His father was a tyrant who didn't want him to study and refused to help him even once during all that time. And yet when he got his degree, he came back home and said to his father . . . You know what he said?'

'What?' she asks.

'Well, he said, "Dad, I . . ." ' And then Robert falls silent and just waves his hand. It's not even a wave, just a shadow of that gesture, signifying utter dejection.

'Come on, what did he say?' she asks.

'Forget it. It doesn't matter now, does it? Did you hear what that fool said about his future?' Robert is mocking me now, but in the way you mock someone you love deeply. '"Future's a word I won't need any more." Shit! The worst thing is I believe him. I believe him because nobody knows him the way I do.'

And that poor sad cunt will never know what I said to my tyrant of a father, who was sometimes a lawyer and

151

sometimes a doctor; for the cunts from New York he was a lawyer, for the ones from California a doctor. Or maybe the other way around. It's unimportant. The beautiful thing is, she'll never know what I said. And Robert doesn't know either, but he's taught me to appreciate the power of an unfinished conversation, which can be resumed naturally and easily after a few hours or even a few days. My real father was a good and gentle man who died when I was six. But a father like that was absolutely worthless, Robert said. 'Forget him. Your father has to be straight out of a Dickens novel. Maybe even a religious fanatic who drove your mother to an early grave. Leave your parents to me.' I soon learned that one of my uncles was a madman who had murdered his wife in a sudden attack of jealousy, that my parents were both alcoholics, and later – this was when we were hustling the girl from Boston – that I didn't have a father at all but was the illegitimate son of a poor washerwoman who knew nothing about my father except that he was a corporal on summer exercises with his regiment. 'The unfortunate child grew up unwanted like a weed and a sore in everybody's eye,' Robert told the poor bitch, pointing at me. Both of them had tears in their eyes.

I dived into the water a couple more times and then went back to where they were sitting.

'I'm sorry,' I said to Robert. 'I shouldn't have said that.'

'It's all right. You don't have to apologize. I'm your friend, you know,' he added after a pause.

I looked at him and smiled sadly, the way you smile when you feel like crying, and Robert answered me with

152

the same kind of smile: there was no strength in it, only the loyalty of one beaten man to another. This was one of those moments when people feel that something special is happening, something they can barely grasp and don't have a name for. Our moment was lifted from *Casablanca*, a film we both liked to see from time to time: the closing scene when Bogey and Claude Rains slowly walk into the fog that covers the airport.

Suddenly we were jolted by a piercing scream. The woman's kid had thrown his ball at a man in a deckchair a few yards away. The man, dressed in khaki shorts and a short-sleeved shirt, was quietly watching children splash around in the water. He had a sweet smile on his face, the kind of smile only a man who's ever known the joys of fatherhood can have. But that smile belonged to the past now: the kid's ball had knocked the man's wig off his head, and his face was red with rage. He held his greyish hairpiece in his left hand, and his right was gripping the boy by the arm; people were shrieking with laughter.

'Where's your father?' the man yelled.

'I won't tell you,' the kid said. I could see from his expression, even though his arm must have hurt terribly, that he was trying to be brave.

'Oh yes you will!'

'I won't!'

'You won't?'

'No!'

When the man placed the kid across his knees to give him a good spanking, I stood up and went over.

'Let him go,' I said. 'Stop molesting that child. Shame on you!'

153

'Is this your kid?'

'Let him go!' I said, pulling the kid out of the man's clutches.

'You should teach him better manners.'

'Why? He's not mine. Just as those hairs aren't yours. You should be ashamed.'

'He's not your kid?'

'I don't think so,' I said. 'I've always wanted daughters only. Like King Lear.'

Something awful bit my hand; when I looked down I saw it was the kid. He met my gaze. Standing with his feet wide apart he was getting ready to hit me. 'Bug off, you sad creep!' he said to me. 'I can take care of myself!'

'See?' the wigless man said, and he nodded with satisfaction. 'The way Americans bring up their kids!'

'Keep calm, sonny,' I said to the kid. My hand was on fire. 'Take your ball and go and play somewhere else.'

The kid had a crew cut; if he hadn't, his hair would have stood on end from sheer anger. 'Next time mind your own bloody business,' he told me.

'Okay.'

He was still looking at me, and I had the impression he was trying to judge his chances of knocking me down. He couldn't decide whether to kick me in the shins or butt me in the belly with his head, a blow Poles call 'the ram'. 'I bet my daddy could kill you,' he said at last.

'Maybe.'

'My dad is awfully strong, you know? Once he beat the hell out of two sailors in Naples. Under a bridge, or maybe in a tunnel. Is that your dog?'

'Yes,' I said.

154

'What's it called?'

'Spot.'

'Like in that story by London?'

'Yes.'

'Okay,' he said, shaking his fist at me. 'Next time remember to mind your own business.' He went off carrying his ball.

'Insolent little brat,' the bald man said, still holding his hairpiece in his hand. 'I should have given him a good thrashing.'

'Better thrash your wig,' I said. 'If I were you, I wouldn't be caught dead wearing something like that. It makes you less attractive to women. I've read that bald men make better lovers. They have more room in their skulls for their hormones.'

I went back to my chair.

'Thank you,' the woman said.

'Not at all.'

'Do you like children?'

'No,' I said. 'Though I like your kid. I admire his nerve. My sister's got a boy just like that.'

'It's hard to bring up a boy when you're alone,' she said, getting up, collecting her things.

'Are you going already?' I asked.

'It's almost six,' she said.

I got up and took the bag from her hand. 'I'm sorry I was so rude. I shouldn't have shouted.'

Looking at her face, I thought that three or four years from now no head would turn when she walked down the street or went into a cinema. It's odd how women's looks suddenly disappear and the women themselves, too, vanish without a trace at the age when men become truly handsome and mature. Women's faces grow cold and grey, and they begin to speak in sharp high voices that have no love, no despair, only a kind of miserable wisdom that prevents them from doing reckless things.

'It's okay, really,' she said. I gave her back the bag and she smiled at me. 'I'm sorry you're having problems.'

'Not any more,' I answered. 'Not since I made up my mind to go.'

She left and I went back to Robert. His skin had taken on a reddish tint, but I knew that tomorrow it would be as pale as ever.

'What did you tell her?' he said.

'Don't worry. Did I get it right earlier?'

'You certainly did.'

'I feel sorry for the dog,' I said.

'Don't think about it.'

'And I feel sorry for her, too. I feel sorry for them all. Tell the dog to leave me alone.'

'Leave him alone,' Robert said to the dog. The dog went away.

'I feel sorry for all of them,' I said again. 'They have just one more summer. That's when they try for the last time, with all the money they've been saving for God knows how many years. Then they disappear and are no longer around. I don't mean they leave or go away. They just vanish. And nobody gives a damn. As if they never existed.'

'If that mood ever strikes you while you're with her, remember to keep your mouth shut. Otherwise you could ruin everything.'

156

'Don't worry.'

'Sometimes I don't know what to expect from you next.'

'Robert,' I said, 'if I had a woman of my own, would I have to talk to her, too?'

'You'd think of something to say.'

'No, I wouldn't. The only thing I'd tell her would be: "Please, I beg you, don't ever talk to me. Don't say a word until the day you decide to leave me."'

'Not bad, not bad at all. One can tell you're talking from personal experience. But you should speak a little more slowly. I have to keep reminding you of that. Right, let's go and eat.'

'Did I do all right?'

'You did indeed. You're great. I told you that long ago, you just don't have enough faith in yourself.'

'It's because of the dog,' I said. 'I can't look at it. I wish everything was over.'

'It almost is,' he said. 'I can feel the money in my pocket. But I've just thought of something. You've got to shout.'

'When?'

'When you refuse to go away with her. Do you see why? People who know they're in the wrong always shout. They want to drown out their thoughts with noise. When a man knows he's wrong and is acting against his own convictions, he starts shouting. Don't forget this. It's very important. A simple psychological trick, but it works. You won't forget?'

'No,' I said. 'I won't.'

When we returned to the hotel, Robert went to sleep. I walked out onto the balcony. I wasn't hungry and I didn't feel like reading; I stood leaning out and looking at the sea. It was dark and quiet. Our hotel was situated a distance from the city, no noises reached us; I could hear the waves come in and die on the hot sand. It's strange how quickly you get used to hearing the sea and how much you begin to depend on it. It would be unbearable, I thought, to go away and never see the sea again. Motionless, I listened to the purring of the waves and watched the lights blink in the distance. I wasn't thinking of the woman or our dog or what I would soon have to do; the sea released me from all thought and feeling, the way alcohol releases other people. It took me a long time to discover the sea had that power, but it was something I found out for myself so it meant a lot to me. How many things are there, I wondered, that a man can discover about himself without anyone's help? Not many; all that shouting Robert talks about drowns out the way we really are and all the gifts we possess, even though we don't possess all that many. So it's a good thing we have at least the sea to look at and listen to. No know-all bastard can change that, or try to; that's what felt so good about looking at the sea.

'Aren't you sleepy?' Robert asked.

'No,' I answered. 'I'm in a philosophical mood. But you go back to sleep.'

'I'm trying to, but I can't.'

'Nerves?'

'No,' he said. 'I was thinking about theatre. And then about something else. Then I started thinking about the dog. It's costing us a pretty penny.'

'How much did it eat today?'

'Two pounds. And it could easily eat twice as much. The butcher at the kosher delicatessen looked at me as if I was crazy when I told him that all that meat was for my dog. What did you eat today?'

'Some soup and a steak. I only spent a pound and a half.'

'This damn beast is costing more than both of us together. Maybe we should get rid of it.'

'It's up to you. You're the director. I'm only going through the motions. I don't even know my part well.'

'One day you'll be a real actor.'

'I wouldn't bet on that,' I said. 'But have it your way.'

'You'd make a good one.'

'My voice is lousy.'

'What do you mean your eyes are lousy? You've got great eyes! Who the fuck told you they were lousy?'

'Nobody said anything about my eyes. I said my voice was lousy.'

'Well, work on it. It's all a matter of training. But you'll never be able to play in a comedy. That's your weak point.'

'Do you mean that what I'm doing now isn't comic?'

'Depends how you look at it.'

'Robert, let's get rid of the dog.'

'No, the dog's not a prop. It's an actor. I've just realized that. It's an actor. You're playing together. And you need it to play out your anger.'

'I can break somebody's head,' I said. 'Even fight a man twice my size. But let's forget about the dog.'

'No. You've got to do something really vile. Something you'll be ashamed of for the rest of your life.'

'The worst part is I have to feel ashamed twice,' I said. 'Both before and after the act.'

'You've got no choice,' Robert said. 'That's why you're so tragic. Oedipus plucked his eyes out so he wouldn't have to see the world. Think in similar terms. Good night.'

At seven in the morning the bouncer came into the room. We were still in bed.

'Listen,' he said, 'I need to talk to you.'

'What about?' Robert asked.

'The deal. I think I'll . . .'

'Okay,' Robert said, 'but not here. There's a café on the next corner. Wait for us there. The woman is staying on the same floor. God forbid she overhears anything. And the coffee they serve here is awful. Go. We'll join you straight away.'

The bouncer left, throwing our dog a timid glance. We dressed quickly and went out into the hall. I was locking the door when I heard a terrible blast: that kid of hers had fired a blank pistol at Robert's ear.

'Don't be afraid, sucker, it's only a toy,' the kid said. 'But I sure gave you a scare! You're chicken, you know.'

It took Robert a moment to regain the power of speech.

'You're chicken!' the kid yelled, reloading his pistol.

'What's your name, sonny?' Robert asked him sweetly.

'Johnny,' the kid said. This time he fired at some old crone. She fell against the wall, white as a sheet. 'Like Johnny Guitar.'

160

'A doctor,' the crone moaned, gasping for breath. 'Get me a doctor, hurry!'

'You'll be all right,' Robert told her. 'Just take a few deep breaths, show more good will to your fellow man, and everything will be tip-top.'

Johnny fired his next shot at a waiter carrying a tray stacked with coffee cups; the loud bang of the shot blended rather nicely with the crash of breaking china.

'You obviously have the wrong approach to children,' Robert added, addressing the crone. Then he wiped his brow and turned to me. 'He says his name is Johnny, but every time I look at him it seems to me he's one of Charles Addams's characters sprung to life. He's the weird boy who's raising a pet pelican in a bottle.'

'He'll end up in the electric chair,' I said.

'A worse end that than. His cellmates will strangle him and tear his body to pieces. All of America will sigh in relief. But imagine how much the country will suffer before that happens.'

When we entered the café, the bouncer was already there, drinking coffee, looking embarrassed.

'Listen,' he said when we sat down at his table, 'I made up my mind. I want out.'

'Oh, you do?' Robert asked. 'Would you mind telling us why?'

'I've had a better offer. My brother and I are going to make chicken coops for the kibbutzim. We know some people who run a carpentry shop, and we can go into business together. We used to build cooling towers with them. Great guys.'

Robert looked as if he was going to split apart. 'Chicken coops? Are you crazy? I'm breaking my neck, so is my partner, her kid shoots at me this morning and I think I'm going to have a heart attack, and you tell me you want to make chicken coops. Why don't you and your brother hatch eggs instead and convert the chicks to the Eastern Orthodox Church before you slaughter them?'

'I don't know how reliable this deal of yours is,' the bouncer said.

'Compared to chicken coops it's rock solid. Don't be a child. We've talked about it, shaken hands on it, so now just leave the rest to us, all right? Trust us. All you have to do is collect your cut when I tell you to. Then you can go ahead and start your chicken farm for all I care.'

'I didn't sleep a wink the last two nights,' the bouncer complained.

'I believe you. He didn't either. But that's your problem. Buy yourself some sleeping pills and don't disturb us any more. We're not magicians. We need time. But hard work and patience always meet their reward. Didn't they teach you that in school? Listen, do you know the story of Bruce, the Irish revolutionary?'

'No.'

'Bruce was a resistance fighter in the struggle against the English. One day he was severely wounded, but he managed to hide in a cave. He was almost certain he was going to die when . . .'

Suddenly our dog growled and we all turned around. The man who had asked us to buy him a beer the day before had no intention of leaving us alone today either. I could see he'd done more heavy drinking last night.

'Buy me a Gold Star and I'll go,' he said. 'I wouldn't bother you but I'm dying for a drink.'

162

'Why pick on us?' Robert asked. 'Aren't there any rich Americans left in town?'

'I need a drink,' the man said, looking at me. It was clear he hadn't forgotten me.

'You won't scrounge one from us,' I said. 'Stop looking for trouble. Didn't you have enough yesterday?'

'I'm not talking to you,' he said. I don't know why he hated me so much; he didn't even try to hide his feelings. Maybe he sensed I felt pity for him, and he couldn't stand that. 'Why don't you shut your trap?' he said to me. 'Shut up!'

'You won't get anything from us,' Robert said. 'What a nerve!'

'Gimme the money for a beer.'

'No. On your way.'

He staggered. I could tell he wanted to slug Robert. I stepped in between them, needlessly, I suppose. He wasn't strong enough to hurt anyone. When his fist hit my arm, the blow was as weak as a child's. The man was about forty, tall, and he'd probably been handsome before he started boozing.

'You know what happens now, don't you?' I asked.

A couple of waiters grabbed him by the shoulders and dragged him out of the café, even though he spat all over them and tried to bite. I didn't watch. One of the waiters was a young bloke who probably spent all his free evenings at the cinema on Ben Yehuda Street where a ticket costs only sixty piastres. Now he had his big moment. I heard his blow connect with the drunk's jaw, then there was quiet.

163

'Lucky us,' Robert said. 'You could say we're as popular as a shithouse during a typhoid outbreak. Do you know him?' he asked the bouncer.

'Like I told you, we were in the army together. That's all I know. He doesn't know me any more.'

'Right, it's all settled. Go home and wait for your cut.'

'You won't con me, will you?' the bouncer asked. 'I don't even know you guys. You won't con me, will you?'

'No,' Robert said. 'For the love of God, no. Ever since Abraham Lincoln died, there hasn't been anyone as honest as us.' He turned to me. 'Imagine, I wanted to create a theatre for the likes of him. A total waste! There are no values left. That's why no tragedy is possible today. Do you understand what I mean?'

'No,' the bouncer said.

'A hundred years ago Art belonged to the aristocracy and the rich. They knew how to care for it. If an actor like Belmondo had appeared on the stage in Paris or St Petersburg, the theatrical director would have packed his bags the next day. Today Art belongs to everyone. And that's why it's dead. I'm a reactionary. But reactionaries have no power today and Art no longer exists. There are TV sets, cars, and washing machines you buy on credit, but there's no Art. And there never will be any. There's only Henry Miller and Sartre. Sartre made the astounding discovery that men's underwear sometimes happens not to be very clean, and for that reason alone Sartre will be immortal. He might even be awarded the Nobel Prize. Have you read today's paper? Do you know if they've given that louse the Nobel Prize yet? They should give him one every week. You know who

164

I'm talking about, don't you? That lousy little shit who read Kierkegaard before he was old enough to understand him. Well? Has he got it yet? Come on, tell me.'

'I don't know,' the bouncer said. 'All I know is the fight between Liston and Clay is scheduled for February. That's all I know, Robert.'

'You and your bloody chicken coops. You ought to read Sartre. That would help you understand your chickens. And I wanted to give you great theatre. Shit, you don't deserve a thing! You've spoiled the whole day for me. Read Sartre, do anything you like, but don't bother us when we're working. Yes, go home and read Sartre. Read him two or three times.'

'When we met in Tel Aviv, you told me you had a foolproof deal, too. And remember what happened?'

'That wasn't my fault. I told you to go and see G. You went to J.'

'J. knew nothing about the deal,' the bouncer said.

'Of course he didn't. I told you to see G. Everything you've ever done isn't worth a shit.'

'Not worth a shit, huh?' The bouncer was indignant. 'I was the one who introduced you to the bellboy in the hotel. That wasn't worth a shit?'

'Nothing you do is worth a shit,' Robert insisted.

'Just make sure everything works out this time,' the bouncer said in a threatening tone. 'You're not gonna roll me.'

They continued wrangling like that for quite a while.

Whenever Robert set up a deal, he was very secretive and never mentioned any names, only the initials J. and G. Everybody knew who J. and G. were, but Robert stuck to his code. That was the way he operated.

'G. still owes me money,' the bouncer said.

'Read Sartre.'

'J. is a thief, too. They threw him in gaol, but what good is that to me? m I supposed to follow him there to get my money or what?'

'Read Sartre,' Robert said. 'Start on him today. And now leave us alone.'

We paid for our coffee and walked down to the beach. She was already there. We rented two deckchairs and went to join her.

'Good morning,' she said.

'Did you sleep well?' Robert asked.

'I heard Johnny gave you a scare this morning.'

'Nothing of the sort,' Robert said. 'He's a lovely child. And so lively, too. I was just like him as a boy.'

While he talked about Johnny and himself, I watched the kid. He was as busy as a one-man band. First he tied a long string to an old man's chair, and when the old fart was about to sit down, he pulled it out from under him. 'The kid's got a healthy sense of humour,' Robert said, watching the old man trying to get up. Then the kid started making mud balls and slinging them at women who didn't want to get their hair wet while swimming. One throw was enough to ruin a ten-dollar hairdo; his aim was true, and his hand never wavered. He engaged in this activity for some time. I calculated that the hairdressers at the Dan Hotel would earn at least a hundred and fifty dollars extra, not including tips. Then he got bored with this game. Suddenly he vanished, and when he reappeared, he had a whole fistful of clothespegs. Later I found out all the hotel laundry done during the night had landed in the sand. Johnny stuck the clothes-pegs behind the waistband of his swimming trunks and went into the water. I wondered what he needed them for, but a little later I could have kicked myself for being so dense. Johnny had been blessed by Nature with an inventive mind, and this time he had come up with a truly magnificent idea: he swam up to people who wore masks and with one swift motion cut off their air supply by attaching the clothespegs to their snorkels; his helpless victims began to suffocate and then tear the masks off their faces; two men lost their masks and never found them again. One of the kid's victims was a rotten swimmer and a lifeguard had to tow him to shore. Everybody started shouting for the police. People were close to a lynching. The man saved by the lifeguard went into hysterics; a crowd gathered around him, and everybody offered the lifeguard advice. The lifeguard lost his head and hit the man in the jaw. The man went spare and demanded the lifeguard's name: he meant to press charges.

'You'll pay for this!' the hysteric yelled.

'I had no choice,' insisted the lifeguard. 'I only did what all the life-saving manuals tell you to do if someone has a fit.'

'You hit me in the face!'

'You had a fit. I had no choice. That's what they taught me on my life-saving course.'

'Excuse me, what did they teach you? What is a lifeguard supposed to do?' a stranger wanted to know. He had a distinguished manner of speaking. 'What are you supposed to do?'

167

'Slap him in the face,' the lifeguard said. 'Like this.'

He slapped the distinguished-sounding stranger in the face, but he must have miscalculated the force of his blow because the man fell to the ground like a bird shot in flight, and he lay there motionless on the sand as the lifeguard leaned over him, shouting, 'That's what they told us to do in the course. I can show you my manual. These are scientific methods and that man shouldn't resent what I did.'

Nobody understood the lifeguard because he was yelling in Hebrew. Little Johnny decided to give him a hand. 'He's right. It was his duty,' little Johnny said.

'Duty!' the lifeguard yelled, grasping at this word. 'Duty! Duty!'

Finally a cop appeared, took down what had happened, and slowly everyone calmed down.

'Johnny, darling,' his mother said when the crowd dispersed and Robert and I managed to free the kid from the lifeguard's clutches, 'why don't you read something for a while? You'd like that, wouldn't you?'

'I'll give you a book,' Robert said.

'Piss on your book,' said little Johnny with true feeling. 'I wanna play with your dog.'

'Of course, sweetheart,' Robert said. 'I'm sure the two of you will get on famously.' Then he turned to me and added softly. 'He's going to kill our dog. We've got to start looking for a new one.'

'What did you say?' the kid asked, eyeing him suspiciously.

'That we have to feed the dog.'

The kid didn't move. He stood in his characteristic stance: feet spread wide apart, his short cropped head lowered and ready to ram you in the belly. His freckled nose was wrinkled in anger. 'I'll tell my dad to break your jaw. He's gonna lick you good. Your doctor is gonna make a hell of a lot of money putting you back together.'

'Tell us something more about your daddy,' Robert said.

'He's big,' Johnny said, stretching his arms to show how tall his dad was and how wide his shoulders were; the man must have been built like Sonny Liston. 'My daddy is big and strong. He's not afraid of anybody. He can kick the hell out of anyone he wants. Once three drunken sailors ganged up on him, he nearly killed them.'

'Really?' Robert asked.

'Really. My dad is strong. He doesn't pick on people, but if someone picks on him, he just . . .' The kid paused and then added, 'It's a good thing all these insurance agencies are around.'

'He pulverized some sailors in Naples,' I explained to Robert. 'In Naples, under a bridge.'

'No, that was another time,' Johnny said. 'What I'm telling you about now happened somewhere else. I can't remember what that goddamn town was called.'

He whistled at our dog, and the two of them scampered away. Robert went for cigarettes. I was smoking the last one. Suddenly she said, 'Give me your cigarette, please.'

I gave it to her. She didn't try to hide her tears. She sobbed helplessly, uncontrollably; people who were strolling past stopped and looked at her with stupid smiles, then walked off reluctantly. Two fat-faced creeps with drooping bellies stopped in front of us and started whispering to one another.

'Move along,' I said.

'What did you say?' one of them said with surprise.

'I said push off.' They left and I held my hand out to her. 'Come. We'll swim out. No need to advertise your problems.'

She got up and, holding hands, we went into the sea. Fifty yards from the shore were the remains of an old unfinished pier. We climbed onto the wet planks and sat down.

'How can I help you?' I asked.

'I'm okay now.'

'Is it something to do with the boy's father?'

'Yes.'

'Johnny's never met him?'

'No. At least I don't think he can remember him. But he'll meet him any day now.'

'Are you sure that's a good idea?'

'No, it's not,' she said, 'but that's why we came here. Johnny's been begging me for so long that I finally gave in. Maybe it would have been best to let him just go on imagining his father the way he has up till now.'

'I think I understand. But maybe you worry too much. I had an uncle who was the worst man you can possibly imagine; he drank, he played cards, and one day he gambled away the house we lived in. At the same time he was a wonderful person. I loved him more than I loved my mother. My father died when I was five.'

'Illness?'

'No, he was killed. Did you ever hear the expression "a nation of thinkers and poets"?'

170

'No.'

'That's the way the Germans liked to describe themselves. Modesty is a wonderful trait. Now they build a million Volkswagens a year and don't think of the past. Oh, perhaps they feel sorry. The Germans feel sorry after every war.'

'Too bad we haven't got any cigarettes,' she said.

'Wait for me here. I'll swim back to shore and bring us some. I'm sure Robert has bought them by now.'

'No, please stay with me. I'm afraid those two fatsos will swim out here and have one more look at me.'

'They couldn't manage it. They probably have hernias and weak hearts and aren't allowed to exert themselves. Lifting a cigarette to their lips is too much for them. Is the boy's father here?'

'Yes, but he hasn't shown up yet. He was supposed to come yesterday. I wrote to him, but maybe something's happened.'

'Look, I don't want to appear nosy. Just tell me what you feel like telling.'

'His father was born here,' she said. 'We met eleven years ago when I visited Israel for the first time. He went back to the States with me, but soon he realized he wasn't able to live away from Israel. He came back here, then he began to miss America. So he returned to the States and started dreaming of Israel. And so it went, on and on. Until one day he left and didn't show up again.'

'America must be a difficult country to live in,' I said. 'Of course, it's no fun being a stranger anywhere.'

'Yes,' she said. 'Maybe it wasn't his fault.'

I was sure it wasn't his fault. I, too, felt homesick. I longed to go back to Poland. Nothing makes you so homesick as being short of cash.

'Do you want to swim back?' I asked after a while.

'No,' she said. 'It's nice sitting here. What was this to be? Some kind of bridge?'

'A pier,' I said. 'A pier with a bar, music, and other night-time pleasures. But then the man who started building it went bankrupt. His parter robbed him blind. His wife left him. One of his kids got bitten by a rabid dog and developed a stammer. The poor bloke got drunk, climbed in his car, and hit some woman. She took him to court; her lawyer claimed that after the accident she couldn't have sex with her husband because it caused her pain. The court awarded her huge compensation so that her husband could afford to sleep with hookers. And the man lost his driving licence. He tried to drown himself, but he was rescued and resuscitated, and because he had no medical insurance, he had to pay for the hospital. Next he tried to gas himself, then he slashed his wrists, then he swallowed a bottle of sleeping pills, but they saved him every time. He was certified insane, so his wife easily got a divorce and married some rich bastard. Finally the poor wretch plunged a knife into his heart and died in terrible pain in a hospital for the destitute.'

'Good god, how do you know all that?'

'I don't,' I said. 'But if you close your eyes, you can improve on anybody's life. Though if you don't like this ending, I can make up a different one: he let a monkey jump on his back and can still be seen from time to time

172

in the company of leprous beggars. A true Hollywood ending.'

'What does he do? I didn't understand you.'

'He got addicted to smoking hashish.'

'I see. Have you ever been to the States?'

'No.'

'You speak with an American accent. You didn't learn that in school, did you?'

'I didn't learn anything at school. I misbehaved so badly that they used to make me stand in a corner with my face to the wall. That was my punishment. You have to admit that under those circumstances I didn't stand a chance of learning anything. Even the gym teacher would throw me out of the door.'

She smiled.

'That's what I wanted,' I said.

'What?'

'To see you smile.'

'Oh, I'm feeling much better now. So where did you learn English?'

'I worked in the desert for a land-surveyor. You know, one of those guys who run around with poles measuring distances and can never get their numbers right. My boss was an American and every day for fourteen hours I listened to him curse. After a while we got used to each other.'

'You worked in the desert . . .' she began.

'Yes,' I said. 'But please don't say it must have been romantic. It wasn't romantic at all. Lots of scorpions and things like that. Lots of snakes, too, so we had to wear boots all the time. And in the evening my boss would bore me with stories about his family. His mother-in-law was an angel, his wife was an angel, his father-in-law was another angel. Fortunately they all died. All he had left was me and his memories. His angel of a mother-in-law died of a heart attack, his angel of a wife died in a car crash, and his angel of a father-in-law drank himself to death. They all flew to heaven.'

'I'm worried about Johnny,' she said.

Suddenly she burst into tears again. I stroked her cheek, remembering to do it clumsily and roughly. You know: a rough man, but a heart of gold. She leaned her head on my shoulder and continued sobbing. I could see she was making an effort to be brave but couldn't help herself.

'Is it something to do with Johnny's father? Something bad?'

'This is going to sound awful, but it would be better for Johnny if his father were dead. Oh, God!'

'God will know what's best for the boy. Don't decide for Him.'

'You're right. I'm sorry.'

'If you have any problems, maybe I can explain things to Johnny for you. I'll come up with some idea for saving the image of his father for him.'

'Will you do that?'

'Of course, I like the boy.'

'You like him?'

'Of course I do. At times I feel like tearing him to pieces, but that's got nothing to do with it. I like to watch him.'

'He likes you, too. And I know why. You resemble the father he's imagined for himself.' She looked at me. 'Or maybe that's why he doesn't like you. Do you understand?'

'No.'

'Hasn't any woman ever told you you're a very attractive man?' she asked. The tone of her voice wasn't pleasant at all.

'No,' I replied. 'Never.'

'Well, then, the women you've had weren't worth a damn.'

I didn't say anything, and, even if I'd wanted, I wouldn't have been able to since she quickly added, 'Please don't be angry. I'm a straightforward person. If I like someone, I don't beat about the bush. I take full responsibility for anything I say.'

I touched her arm. 'Are you sure you allow others the same rights as yourself?'

'Of course.'

'Then listen. I like you, too. I think you're very pretty.'

'Oh, oh,' she said.

'Oh, oh,' I repeated, nodding.

'Really?'

'Really. Otherwise I wouldn't be sitting here with you. No one gives a damn about the tears of an ugly woman. If an ugly woman begins to cry, you tell her she's got beautiful eyes and walk away. Too bad, but that's the way men are. As you probably know. What's your name?'

'Mary. I guess it's Miriam in Hebrew.'

'I prefer Mary,' I said.

'What's yours?'

'Jacob.'

'And in Hebrew?'

'Ya'akov. But the problem is I'm a Catholic.'

'Is it tough being a Catholic here?' she asked.

'No. If people like you, you can get along anywhere. And people here take pride in being able to offer work and shelter to someone of a different faith. At least, some of them do. There are some who don't like Catholics, but that's not surprising. Let's go back. I'm dying for a cigarette.'

'Okay,' she said.

When we reached our spot on the beach, I looked at my watch; it was six o'clock. Robert had gone to the hotel. He'd left me a packet of cigarettes and a note: 'Take it easy, don't hurry things. And don't forget about your anger and inner turmoil. Little Johnny let our dog loose in a kosher butchers. He ate a lot of meat. Big losses. We have to go to the police station tomorrow. Take your time and remember the German saying, "Patience brings roses." I'll wait for you in the hotel. Robert.' We both lit up and then went to change. I took off my swimming trunks and placed them next to my clothes outside the shower stalls. When I finished showering, I towelled myself and was about to reach for my trousers when a small, quick hand darted out from behind the wall and grabbed them. I didn't have to check to know that my swimming trunks and shirt had disappeared, too. Clutching a small towel wrapped around my waist, I leaned over the partition and called out to Mary: 'Can you hear me?'

'Yes.'

'I'm totally naked. Johnny swiped my clothes.'

'Your clothes?'

'Yes,' I said. 'I have a wet cigarette in my mouth, but that's all I've got.'

'I'll give him a spanking,' she promised.

'Later. Right now can you lend me your bathing suit, please? I've got to get back to the hotel.'

'In a lady's bathing suit?'

'I'll say I've developed breasts,' I answered cheerfully. 'Or that I'm a hermaphrodite. It can be quite funny. I don't care. I just want to put something on.'

She tossed me her bathing suit and I squeezed into it hastily. I overheard two men talking about me: one said that in California there were lots of men who were attracted solely to members of their own sex, and the other said that he had once been to a men's beauty parlour and that it was absolutely disgusting.

Looking at me pointedly, they both expressed concern for the future of the American nation, which had so quickly ceased to be a nation of pioneers and had completely degenerated. Then the first one told his friend that if he had read the Bible he wouldn't be so surprised, since such things were already known in Sodom and Gomorrah. As well as ancient Greece. The other man said he felt insulted to be talked to like some kind of ignoramus; they left quarrelling.

'Well, Johnny,' I said to myself, 'I think you have a surprise coming. And I don't think you're going to like it.'

'Hey, have you changed yet?' Mary called out.

'I'll be the prettiest girl on the beach,' I yelled, 'as cute as Debbie Reynolds.'

'Maybe I'd better go look for Johnny.'

'Don't bother. It won't do any good. He didn't steal my things in order to let you find them. Anyway, he's probably made them into a sail or something else by now.'

'Johnny's a monster,' she said when I walked out. 'I'll give him a good spanking today. On his last birthday he set the house on fire and we had to call the fire brigade. My mother almost had a heart attack.' She came up to me and kissed me on the cheek. She did it sweetly and naturally, as if she were my sister. 'But don't be angry at him, please.' Her eyes filled with tears again. 'It's all my fault. I don't know how to bring him up.'

'I'm not angry,' I said. 'I never thought I'd look this good in a lady's swimsuit. The floral design is exquisite. I'm sure Robert will appreciate it, too.'

'You're very nice, you know? I like you.'

That's how it all began. She was only a step away; I held out my hand. We exchanged one timid kiss, then another. The two who had quarrelled over Sodom and Gomorrah had apparently made up, and now, watching, they started to discuss an Ingmar Bergman film in which two sisters display rather excessive feelings for each other.

'Pipe down, gentlemen,' I said. 'Ingmar Bergman is a pipsqueak. That's what Orson Welles said about him and I trust Welles's judgment. This lady, by the way, is my illegitimate daughter.'

'Such things were common practice in ancient Greece,' the classicist said, as they moved away.

The other one stopped as if struck by lightning.

'I'm fed up with you and your classical education!' he yelled. 'Just because I let you lecture me on the Greeks and the Bible, you think I don't know who screwed me on our last deal?'

'And you gave me a bad cheque,' the other cried, close to tears. 'If I pressed charges, you'd be in jail. It's no joke!'

They turned in separate directions and went their own ways.

Robert left, taking the dog with him. He was spending the night at the bouncer's apartment so I would have our room to myself. I sat on the balcony, reading Chekhov. I read him all the time, lugging the heavy volumes wherever I went; they were a present from Robert, who also gave me a lecture on Chekhov's greatness. He was right. There are many great writers, but Chekhov is more than that; he's a friend. It always surprises me how cruel he can be at times. I think he was unaware of his own cruelty; it wasn't something he aimed for, which is why he seems so vicious at times. 'His imagination was completely lacking anger,' Robert said. He had his own ideas of how to stage Chekhov, and he used to talk about them often and at length. The last time he enlarged on his theories was in the Jaffa jail – his audience was a beggar who used to beat his children with an iron rod. I think the beggar understood the lecture; he broke into tears when Robert recited parts of *The Cherry Orchard*. That happens, too.

Robert was a fanatic when it came to theatre. In the jail he always performed for other inmates. He had fixed

179

rates for his artistic services: one cigarette for the *Macbeth* monologue, which begins, 'Tomorrow, and tomorrow, and tomorrow,' if delivered in Polish, two if in English. The balcony scene from *Romeo and Juliet* belonged to the cheaper classical repertoire: one smoke for the two of us, since I played Juliet. These were the more expensive pieces. The modern stuff I did alone and for much lower rates. Robert never attempted anything contemporary; he was a priest of High Art. I remember how once he and a smuggler, who in his youth had been a member of an amateur theatre company in Cairo, came to blows while playing *Faust* together; or rather how Robert started beating the other inmate for overacting his role and being too theatrical. When we finally managed to pull them apart, Robert continued to upbraid him, screaming that while on stage an actor should tie the wings of his soul. I was much more modest than Robert; I usually acted out scenes from films. My greatest success was impersonating Goofy. Naturally, I had more cigarettes than Robert, so he would smoke mine and bitch about the degeneration of public taste and the stupidity of films.

Robert had come to Israel from Poland. His big wish was to create Art. He found employment in a Tel Aviv theatre but they fired him almost immediately because he quarrelled ceaselessly with all the actors, criticizing them for following the Stanislavski method, which he found loathsome; this was rather strange since he admired both Elia Kazan and Lee Strasberg. He made such a nuisance of himself and got on everybody's nerves so much that they gladly got rid of him at the first opportunity. He then convinced two con men to start a cabaret show, but the first night they succeeded in insulting everybody: religious zealots and agnostics, fresh immigrants and native Israelis, the press, the army, and God knows who else. The two con men grabbed a taxi and left Tel Aviv straight after the performance, pocketing the night's take and leaving Robert alone to face three trials, including one for not paying for the building they had rented for the show. This was how he ended up in jail. He wrote to his erstwhile partners, begging them to help him out, but they ignored his pleas. He began counselling other inmates, explaining the niceties of the law to them. I met him soon after, sitting on his cot, fat and grubby, giving legal advice to a blind man.

'Okay, tell me what happened,' Robert asked him.

'Well, I kind of felt a hankering,' the blind man answered.

'A hankering to screw your own daughter?'

'I just wanted to help her fasten her bra,' the blind man explained. 'She asked me to.'

'How often did that happen?'

'Well, now and again.'

'You've got nothing to worry about,' Robert told the blind man cheerfully. 'All you have to do is tell the judge you didn't see who you were screwing. You're blind, aren't you?'

All the inmates roared with laughter, while the blind man burst into tears. Then Robert met a guy who could make puppets, and so – still in the slammer – they started preparing a puppet show together. When Robert was released, he somehow raised the cash to bail the puppet-maker out. The two of them visited me in the hotel where I was staying and turned my room into their workshop. They even made me help them. We worked on those puppets for three weeks, eating only one meal a day: hummus, which the puppet-maker got at an Arab restaurant. When the puppets were finished, Robert persuaded the owner of an articulated truck to drive them around; the truck owner became their new partner. They gave two shows in kibbutzim close to the Syrian border; during the third show, devout Jews overturned the truck, burned all the puppets, then chased Robert and his pals for half a mile, showering curses on their heads and spitting on them. The owner of the truck brought charges against Robert, who got locked up again.

I was in bad shape then, too. I couldn't obtain a work permit, but I managed to land a job on a building-site in Bat-Yam, and I worked there for a while. One day I slipped and broke my arm; a compound fracture. The doctor who set my arm said I would have to wear a cast for six weeks. I didn't have any money for food, and I was really low. An asthmatic burglar staying in the same hotel lent me money for the rent and food. He was a nice bloke, born in one of the Arab countries; spoke French like a born Parisian and was rather proud of it. He hated General de Gaulle; said he looked like a fairground barker and would ruin France. He used to rage that De Gaulle had never been to the front and had cribbed his book on the need for mechanization of the French army from General Guderian; that he had spent the whole war in London spouting drivel over the radio while he should have been fighting the Germans. The burglar went under the nickname of 'De Gaulle.'

Soon afterwards the real De Gaulle put down the paratroopers'' rebellion, while the 'De Gaulle' I knew was arrested for having robbed the cash register at a kosher co-op. A few days later the police arrested me: some squealer must have told them De Gaulle had given me money. That's how all three of us found ourselves in the Jaffa nick: De Gaulle, Robert, and me. One day I was about to be taken to the examining magistrate and a guard wanted to handcuff me.

'Come on,' I said. 'I don't need those. I'll go quietly without the bracelets.'

'It's an order,' the guard said.

'Nothing doing,' I said. 'I don't care.'

He tried to grab my hand, but I pushed him away. So he went back to the guardroom and I heard him ask the sergeant what he should do.

'You've got to answer violence with violence,' the sergeant told him, though I never learned what violence he meant. They came back and beat me unconscious. As soon as I opened my eyes, Robert said, 'I have a great idea.'

'You're not the only one,' I said. 'Every hustler in this jail has a great idea.'

'I've figured out what to do with you.'

'You have? What?'

'Thanks to you, we'll both be rich!'

'Nobody's ever become rich thanks to me except for one Hungarian. I got hit by a car and the insurance was paid to him because his name was similar to mine. I never found him.'

'He disappeared into the whirlpool of life,' Robert said. 'But your money won't bring him luck. He'll slip on a banana skin one day coming down the stairs and become a pathetic invalid. He'll sing on street corners and some day you'll pass by and throw him a penny. He'll recognize you, but you won't recognize him. And then he'll suffer even more.'

'Maybe so.'

'You handled yourself nicely in the fight.'

'Then how come I've got these on?' I asked, lifting my hands to show him the handcuffs.

'You kept your head high and proud,' he said. 'I thought, that's how Fabrice del Dongo must have looked on his way to his execution.'

'I didn't keep it high very long. As you probably noticed, they mainly kicked me in the arse.'

'How can Jews act like that?' a pimp complained in a bitter voice. He was handcuffed to Robert; our conversation was taking place in the back of a police van on our way to the magistrate's office. 'Jews, who for so long have been beaten themselves. A man comes here out of idealistic reasons, full of enthusiasm and the best intentions, and before he's even had a chance to look around, the police grab him. And this is the Jewish state we've been waiting for for two thousand years.'

'Well?' Robert asked me. 'What do you say?'

'What do you want me to do?'

'Only what you've always wanted to do yourself. You wanted to be an actor, didn't you?'

'How did you guess?'

'That's my business.'

'I see,' I said. 'I'm not supposed to know too much. Just like in the stories by that guy who wrote *Guys and Dolls*. You're Spanish John, right?'

'No, Little Isidore. And that bastard over there,' he said, pointing to the cop guarding us, 'is really Harry the Horse.'

'Better watch it, or you'll get an additional charge for insulting a police officer,' the cop said.

'So you've read the book, too?' I asked.

'Sure,' the cop said. 'I just read how Harry the Horse and Big Butch went to crack a safe, and Big Butch took his one-year-old kid with him because he didn't have anyone to leave him with.'

'You want me to act?' I asked Robert.

'Yes, but for a very limited audience.'

'Who'll pay me?'

'Don't worry. Everything'll be paid for. Leave it all to me; money will be no problem. You don't mind being paid in American dollars, do you?'

'No, not at all.'

Soon afterwards De Gaulle was transferred to the Akko penitentiary, where he was to serve out a long sentence, while Robert and I gave our first performance. Everything went perfectly; our first client was the American girl who ended up in a nuthouse. That was over a year ago; I remembered it now as I leaned over the balcony rail. The sea in the distance looked misty and dead. I could tell the damned wind was coming and that it wouldn't leave the city in peace. It was half past ten; I knew I wouldn't be alone much longer. Thinking of the wind, which would be on us tomorrow, I didn't feel like reading any more; I didn't even feel like going into the room. I thought of minor, unimportant things; my mind was a total shambles and I couldn't concentrate on anything. All of a sudden I remembered the day Stalin died. Then I thought of the day Patterson beat Johansson, and of winning a bet from someone who never paid up; then I recalled how a certain rich but tightfisted man had hired me as a driving instructor for his wife, though he knew I didn't have a teaching permit and that he wouldn't collect any insurance if his wife wrecked the car.

'Can you drive?' he asked me the first day after treating me to a glass of warm soda water with no fizz in it.

'Yes.'

'Do you drive well?'

'Yes.'

'What sort of make did you drive last?'

'A Wright.'

'What's that?'

'A diesel truck. Fifteen tons. Five gears and a reducer.'

'Have you had any accidents?'

'One.'

His face was shining with sweat; he was worried about his damn car – an old Chevy – but at the same time he was too cheap to part with a few pounds more and hire a professional instructor. I watched him, the half-full glass of warm soda water in my hand, while he trembled and sweated.

'Will you be careful?'

'That's something women usually ask,' I said. 'Of course I will.'

186

'You look as if you enjoyed risky driving.'

'I just look that way.'

'Do you really drive well?'

'I drove you around a bit, so you should know.'

'It's hard to tell after one ride.'

'I can drive you around again.'

'It'd be a waste of gas,' he said. 'It's just as hard to tell after two rides. It's hard to tell anything these days. My partner was the best man there ever was, then he started gambling and didn't stop until he gambled everything away. God, I lost a fortune because of him. You just can't tell anything these days.'

So I started teaching his wife and she was making good progress, but whenever I came to pick her up for her lesson, I could see she'd been crying. Finally, she told me her husband suspected she was having an affair with me and would kick up terrible rows and come close to a heart attack. Neither of us was attracted to the other. Whenever I made a suggestion, she'd say, 'Don't teach me what to do,' even though that was exactly what I was paid for. Or, rather, was supposed to be paid for. Each time I came to collect my fee, her husband would pretend he had no small notes; if I reminded him the next day, he would shout at me not to bother him with such trifles since he had a bad heart – so bad, in fact, that the doctors had stopped hiding it from him. He continued to treat his wife so dreadfully that finally one day she and I overcame our mutual repugnance. After that I never went back to their home. I couldn't bear the thought of seeing her again. She kept gobbling sweets all the time, even when she was behind the wheel; she would break a chocolate bar in half and with a heavy sigh push both pieces into her mouth. After that her husband hired a highly recommended professional instructor. The instructor wrecked the car, and both he and the man's wife ended up in the same hospital. Dark forces had conspired against the husband, Robert said.

It was eleven. When the khamsin blows, you close all doors and windows, but I opened the balcony door to go back into the room. At exactly the same moment that I opened the balcony door, she opened the door to my room. We stopped and looked at each other.

'Close the door,' I said. 'That damn wind has started.'

'I couldn't sleep,' she said. 'I knocked, but you didn't hear me. So I thought you must be sitting out on the balcony.'

'You won't be able to sleep now anyway. When the khamsin comes, nobody sleeps much.'

'Where's Robert?'

'He's not here tonight.'

'I see.' She liked to smile, something I liked about her. 'His ageing mother cabled him that she's not feeling well?'

'No. I told him to get the hell out because I was waiting for you.'

'So I didn't surprise you?'

'No. I hate surprises. I fear them more than anything. The only thing that brings joy is something you want and have been waiting for.'

'Quite a philosophy.'

'No. I just knew we both wanted the same thing.'

'That's nice. Listen, you could also say that there isn't much happiness in the world, so you shouldn't hesitate doing something you feel some good might come from.'

'You took the words right out of my mouth. All I can do is say them again.'

'Listen, why do I like you so much? Maybe you can explain that to me.'

'No. But that explains why you came.'

'Shouldn't I slam the door and leave?'

'We'd lose one night,' I said. 'And I have just enough money to stay here a few more days. Then I'll have to move. By the way, did you give Johnny a spanking?'

'Yes. He traded your pants for a jackknife with a corkscrew. Johnny says it's a very good jackknife. I brought it with me. I thought you should have it.'

She gave me the Swiss Army knife.

'Thank you,' I said. 'Actually I've always wanted one. What about my shirt?'

'He traded it for some kind of lizard.'

'Maybe it'll become friends with my dog.'

'No. It was a stuffed lizard. Next Johnny traded it for a pack of cigarettes. I brought you those, too.'

The cigarettes were Russian; thick as a finger, with cardboard filters.

'I haven't smoked one of these in years,' I said. 'Only Johnny could have come across them here.'

'I'm glad you think so highly of my son.'

'Want to try one?'

'Sure. Then what?'

'Let's have a smoke first,' I said. 'It'll soothe my nerves.'

189

'Actually it's me who should be tense, not you.'

'Not at all. It's me who's afraid.'

'Afraid of what?'

'Disappointing you,' I said. 'And you can't imagine how afraid. I'm not eighteen. This country and this climate have taken their toll.'

'Listen,' she said. She liked that word. 'Listen, I can go if you want. It's just my luck that in this country, where everybody is so goddamn virile, I should be attracted to you.'

'Please stay. Maybe I'll muster the courage. Good cigarettes, aren't they?'

'I never knew plain tar could taste this good.'

'Yes,' I said. 'The Russians have lots of good things. In Poland they never stopped telling us how good their scientists were.'

'What will we do when we finish smoking?'

'I'll tell you something about my childhood. I once had a friend who experimented on frogs. The frogs really hated that. That was in Poland.'

I fell silent.

'Is that your only memory from Poland?' she asked after a terribly long pause, when she must have lost all hope of my continuing the conversation.

'Actually the only thing I really remember from Poland is Khrushchev's face,' I said.

'You're a very strange lover.'

'I know. Once for three nights in a row I explained the construction of a steam engine to some girl. It didn't get me very far. But apparently I was very cheeky as a boy. You'll have to excuse me for a moment. This room doesn't have a toilet.'

190

'Okay,' she said.

I went out into the corridor. There was a buzz in my ears and a total void in my mind. I went down to the reception desk and called Robert from there. When I heard his voice, brisk and eager, I felt a little better.

'Bobby, quick,' I said. 'I've forgotten how it goes after the initial nonsense. It's because of the khamsin. Why don't we wait a few days?'

'Are you crazy? Think how much we're paying for that bloody hotel room. We can't wait, damn you.'

'Then what am I supposed to do now?'

'Don't touch her yet. Tell her what you're going to do to her, but keep away. Wait until she gets so hot she can't stand it.'

'What if she doesn't get hot?'

'She will. No woman can resist for long if you tell her what you intend to do to her. Even St Theresa of the Infant Jesus would have given in. Can't I ever leave you alone? You're like a child, you know?'

'Okay,' I said, putting down the receiver. I went to the hotel bar and drank a beer and listened to two German Jews talking about Goethe.

'He was a great man,' one of them said.

'What do you mean great? He was the greatest!'

'And so cheerful,' the first one gushed.

'He was our greatest poet,' the second one said.

They were both corpulent and elegantly dressed; I was certain they had spent the war in Switzerland or in the States. I looked at my thin face and bleached hair in the mirror over the bar, gulped down the rest of my beer, and turned to them: 'Das beste, was Goethe geschrieben hat, ist *An American in Paris*, meine Herren.'

I bowed and went upstairs. She was standing by the closed window, taking deep breaths. Her forehead was covered with sweat, but that didn't make her any less attractive. Or maybe she wasn't perspiring. Maybe it was only my imagination.

'It's all because of this wind,' I said. 'I'll tell you what happened once in Haifa, when after four days of khamsin . . .'

'I think it's time you shut up,' she said.

'No. I'll decide what comes when. Nothing I desire will pass me by, but I want it to last a long, long time. So that I'll never forget. First I want to think about it, then talk about it, and only then do it.'

'You haven't said anything yet.'

'But I'm going to now. I'm thinking you'll be naked soon and that while I'm undressing you, something may rip. I'm thinking that your breasts are small and your legs strong. And I know your belly is flat and hard. And that afterwards we'll lie next to each other smoking the cigarettes Johnny contrived to get us. And I'm sure we'll speak softly to each other, even though we could speak quite loudly because we're all alone. We'll both be a little uncomfortable. I'll feel your hair on my lips.'

'Don't say anything more.'

'No. I'll go on talking. I'll talk until we both go mad. I'm thinking of your belly, whether it's strong and hasn't been disfigured by Johnny. Maybe it has tiny light scars which I'll be able to feel with my fingertips. I hope so. Maybe I can kiss them once you stop feeling shy. And soon my shyness will also disappear and you, too, will be able to kiss me. And then we'll start again, and the whole room, the bed, everything will have your smell. Not mine, but yours. But until I say that one important word, this is all.'

'I have to leave Israel,' she said.

'So leave. Go wherever you like, remember me only as long as it brings you joy.'

'What if afterwards nothing brings me joy?'

'No man should be so conceited as to believe no other man can replace him.'

'Do you believe that?'

'No.'

'Neither do I.'

'Don't think about it now,' I went on. 'Think what I've been telling you. Think of me taking off your dress very, very slowly, and other things. Think only of that.'

'I love you, you know?' she said. 'I'm glad I said it first. I really am. Did you hear me? I said it first. Will you remember that?'

Robert showed up at the beach at about ten. He looked dreadful. It turned out the bouncer had only one bed and they had had to share it. What's more, the bouncer's girlfriend had dropped in unexpectedly and kicked up a row when she found them in bed together. Somehow they managed to calm her, but then had to share the bed with her, too. The dog slept stretched across their feet.

'The bouncer's worried about his money,' Robert said. 'He kept me awake half the night talking about it.'

'He'll get his cut,' I said.

'I've got a new bride for you.'

'Oh, have you?'

'We'll have to start on her as soon as we finish with this one. She's arriving from the States on the fifteenth and going straight to Tveriah. A bellboy I know told me.'

'But you had to phone him, didn't you?'

'What's the difference? As soon as we finish with this one, we'll go to Tveriah.'

'No,' I said. 'It's too hot over there this time of year. Around 120B in the shade. I'll suffocate.'

'You'll be okay. I hear she's a very nice girl. We have to start looking for a new dog. There's a bulldog I'd like, but the owner wants eighty pounds. That's too much.'

'You won't get a pedigree for less.'

'I'll try.'

'Spot cost us a hell of a lot of money, too.'

'But just think what a dog he is,' he said. 'Like a forest fire or a typhoon.'

I glanced at Spot; little Johnny was chasing him.

'I can't think about him,' I said. 'Every time I see him, I begin to feel dizzy. The dog we had before was nothing compared to this one.'

'Yes, Spot is an exceptionally lovable beast. But it can't be helped.'

'Let's leave out that part.'

'No, that's impossible. We might just as well pack our bags and get the hell out of here. Remember, I'm the one responsible for the whole deal. Don't worry. You'll have plenty of rest when we get to the Sea of Galilee. Everything will be fine. Just think: you, your despair, the woman you love, the lake Jesus walked across . . . Listen, that's not work, that's pleasure. You can quote from the New Testament to her. Maybe some passage

194

from St Paul's First Epistle to the Corinthians, the one on love and charity. A historical spot, love, Arabs shooting at night, your despair, a tornado of sensuality; it should be child's play.'

'Oh, shut up,' I said. 'Even here it's too hot to breathe. I don't want to think of Tveriah.'

'Take it easy. You don't know how to enjoy yourself. How are things going? All right?'

'Yes.'

'See? I told you.'

'You were right,' I said. 'You proved to me what human genius is capable of.'

'Good. I'll go and talk to the bouncer now and try to convince him to back us again. Though I'm afraid he'll be reluctant to risk any more money.'

'We don't need him. When we pull off this job, we should have enough money for Tveriah.'

'I don't think it's a good idea for us to finance ourselves. I'm sure everything'll work out, but what if it doesn't? It's always better if somebody else takes the loss. The same as with film production.'

'Only no one will give us an Oscar, no matter how good we are,' I said. 'And that's the bitter truth.'

'You're an actor, not a star. Remember that. Anyway, Chaplin didn't get an Oscar either.'

'But he got American dollars in Swiss bank accounts. And all he has to pay is four per cent income tax.'

'God willing, one day you'll be wallowing in money, too. Okay, I'm going. Think of the Sea of Galilee. You'll have to be in the depths of despair. They go for that. Despair above all. Think about it.'

'Think about it yourself,' I said.

Robert left. Soon afterwards I heard a piercing scream, which must have reached the highest heavens. Little Johnny's sense of humour had led him too far this time: when some lady swam out to sea on an inflatable rubber mattress, he punctured it with his knife, letting all the air escape; the mattress sank almost immediately. I could see the lifeguard holding Johnny under his arm and a crowd trying to resuscitate the poor woman. The lifeguard began walking in my direction, as unrelenting as fate.

'Is this your kid?' he asked, trembling with anger.

'It's awfully hot,' I said. 'Ask me a simpler question.'

'Do you know what I'm going to do now?'

'I have no idea.'

'I'm going to whack his ass so hard he'll have to crawl on his belly for a week. Everybody's had enough of him!'

'He's a good kid,' I said. 'Let him go, or the blood will rush to his poor little head.'

'Are you responsible for him?'

'Yes.'

'Are you absolutely sure?'

'That's right.'

He let go of little Johnny, who then managed to bite his captor somewhere near the liver. The lifeguard threw down his fancy hat with a brass anchor, the word LIFEGUARD stitched on it.

'I'm talking to you as a private person now,' he said to me. 'Get up from that deck chair.'

'It's too hot,' I said. 'Come back when the khamsin stops blowing.'

196

'Be a man!'

The tone of his voice was so imploring that I had to oblige. He hit me in the jaw with such force that I fell back on the chair, breaking it to pieces. Then he lost his balance and tumbled down; I grabbed him by the hair and kicked him in the belly. He gasped, but managed to hit me once more. I, too, managed to land a blow with the last of my strength. Then we both sat on the sand, breathing hard.

'I'm afraid we won't be able to continue,' I said. 'I'm out of breath. It's because of this bloody wind.'

'You're right,' he said. 'I feel kind of weak myself today. What I need is a cup of strong coffee.'

'Your legwork is lousy. That's why you lost your balance.'

'And you don't know how to kick. You were aiming at my gut, but you got me in the groin.'

'It's too bad I don't know karate,' I said. 'If I did, I could kill you by hitting your Adam's apple with the edge of my hand.'

'Sure. If I let you,' he said, rubbing his belly. 'But I could dodge your blow and then hit you right between the eyes. The nasal bone would break and knife into your brain. Instant death.'

'Karate is a clever art.'

'But you have to learn it well. Another good move is to hit someone in the solar plexus with the tips of your fingers. But you have to be careful not to break your fingers. It's best to wrap a hanky around your hand. Real tight.'

We fell silent. We were both breathing hard; the lifeguard massaged his belly, I massaged my jaw.

197

'I lost my job because of this kid,' he said. 'I just couldn't take it any more. I've been following him around for the past three days, but there's no way to keep him out of mischief. Yesterday he managed to get hold of a magnifying glass and set fire to guests'' pockets, the pockets they kept their money in, of course. As I was carrying him just now, I got so angry something snapped in me. I lost my job, but I don't give a damn.'

'You'll find a new one,' I said.

'Fat chance. The season's almost over. All the hotels already have lifeguards. I won't find anything.'

'You should go to Eilat,' I said.

'What for?'

'I know some people down there. They could find you a job in Solomon's mine. Or in the harbour.'

'I prefer the harbour.'

'It can be arranged.'

'I'm willing to give it a try,' he said. 'You don't have to pay taxes in Eilat. Can you really help me?'

'Sure. When you get there, ask for Abram Szafir. He's a wonderful guy. I stayed with him two years ago. He'll help you find something. Can you play cards?'

'Of course.'

'Then don't have second thoughts about going. A good player is worth his weight in gold there. Everybody's bored stiff; playing cards is the only entertainment.'

'Will you write me a note to your friend?'

I wrote a note and gave it to him. The lifeguard picked up his fancy hat and handed it to me.

'Give it to the kid. Actually, I never wanted to be a lifeguard.'

He left. I got up, too, and started searching for Johnny. When I found him, he was busy building a sandcastle on an old gentleman in the sand. The old man was watching him with a kindly expression.

'You should buy him a toy,' the old man said. 'Maybe a spear gun, something like that.'

'You don't know him,' I said. 'The only toy he'd enjoy playing with is a flamethrower. Come, Johnny. Come along, dear. There's something we have to talk about.'

He stood up and followed me.

'Yesterday you traded away my shirt and my trousers,' I said. 'Then you let our dog into a meat shop and the poor animal ate so much it hasn't been able to eat since. The chair the lifeguard broke throwing me on will cost at least thirty pounds. I just want you to know the holy saints don't shower money on me from the sky, and I don't expect them to start anytime in the near future.' I gripped his shoulder and turned him towards me. 'The fact is I'm a poor man, John. I'm sorry to have to tell you that.'

'You mean you don't have any money?'

'No, John. I never had any.'

'Try making some.'

'That's excellent advice, John. But it so happens I haven't got any money now.'

He held out his hand. 'I'm sorry.'

'That's all right,' I said.

'Listen, do you want to sell your dog?'

'No, Johnny. Spot isn't for sale.'

'I'd like to have him,' he said. 'He's a good dog. And Americans love dogs.'

'Yes, I know. Americans love dogs more than any other nation does. But Spot isn't for sale.'

'Spot would like it in America.'

'I know, John. But I can't sell you my dog. It's too late now, and it can't be changed.'

'Too late?'

'Maybe I've expressed myself badly. But Spot has to stay with me and that's it. Spot is my only friend.'

'How about Robert?'

'Listen, John. Spot isn't going anywhere. End of story.'

'There is a way out,' Johnny said. 'I think I know how to get that dog to the States.'

'What do you mean?'

'Can I talk to you man to man?'

'You can try.'

'It seems that my mom loves you, you know?'

'I know,' I said.

'Do you love her, too?'

'Yes I do, John.'

'Listen,' he said, 'did either of you think what is gonna happen when my daddy finds out? He's gonna kick the shit out of you!'

'I'll have to defend myself. That's all I can do.'

He looked at me with a crooked smile. 'Man, you don't stand a chance!'

'Even if I don't, I'll still have to fight. Wouldn't you?'

'Sure I would. But I feel sorry for you. I know my daddy. Look, have you kissed my mom?'

'Yes, I have.'

'And she kissed you?'

200

'She's kissed me, too.'

'Then it looks real bad for you. Listen, just don't tell my daddy that. I know it's not right, but I worry for you all the same. If my daddy finds out, he's gonna kill you. As things stand, he might do it anyway. Listen, did I ever tell you about the time some bums picked a fight with him in a bar on Russian Hill in San Francisco?'

'No.'

'Actually there isn't much to tell. When he was done with them, they were barely breathing. Anyway, remember what I just told you.'

'Okay. I will.'

He turned to leave, then stopped. 'Actually, you're okay, you know? You weren't bad in that fight with the lifeguard. You're quick.'

He walked away, taking the dog with him. All in all, a lovable kid. Then I groaned softly; the lifeguard had landed a few good ones. I felt so lousy that I decided to get drunk that evening. I thought the thief crucified next to Jesus must have been as meek as a lamb compared to little Johnny. No doubt about it. And then, after a while, I began to think about Johnny's father, and that made me feel even worse.

But I didn't get drunk in the evening. I lay in bed with her head resting on my shoulder as we watched the sea, motionless and silent, through the open balcony door. The moon seemed glued to a sky suffocating under a heavy fog; the world looked empty and dark.

'When this damned wind stops blowing, he'll start talking again,' I said.

'Who? You mean the sea?'

'Yes.'

'Why do you think of the sea as masculine? English grammar is of a different opinion.'

'I don't give a damn. I just wish he'd start talking again. That's all.'

'California is by the sea, too,' she said softly.

'Don't.'

'Wouldn't you like to go there?'

'No.'

'Every time I look at you and Johnny . . .'

'Then stop looking at us. I'm not going to California.'

'But you want to go to Australia.'

'I have a job there.'

'Listen, you think there aren't jobs in America? Don't be ridiculous.'

'I'm too old for America. It scares me. I love America too much to risk disappointment. It probably seems strange to you, but that's the way I feel. I'm a Pole. All Poles are cripples. America doesn't need cripples.'

'Why do you call yourself that?'

'Because it's true,' I said. 'And it can't be changed. I wanted to be an actor once, but it didn't work out. I didn't finish school, so the Actors'' Studio rejected me. I could have tried again some years later, but my nerves gave out. I started writing, but that didn't get me very far, either, damn it. Then I came here, because I wanted to see the place immortalized in the Bible. I haven't got a work permit, so I have to report to the police every two weeks and explain how I manage to survive. But soon it'll all be over.'

'Calm down. Take it easy. It's all because of the wind. It's making everybody crazy. You'll come with me.'

'I never said that.'

'You will, tomorrow.'

'Listen,' I said. I, too, had started saying 'listen'. She and Johnny had taught me that. 'Listen, it's not only that. I'm a loser. And I'd keep on losing on the other side of the ocean. I like clear situations. For me, Australia is the end of the road, and I know it. In America it would take me more time to free myself from new illusions.'

'I don't care about America or Australia. I care about us.'

'There's nothing we can do,' I said. 'Listen, when you're twenty years old, you despise compromises. Later, you begin to accept them because there isn't any other way. Then one day you learn to feel happy just because the woman you love is alive somewhere. And who she is with ceases to be important. You're happy because she's alive and breathing.' I paused a long time, then added, 'And that's the onset of old age, which comes too soon.'

'Have you had so much love in your life you can reject this love?'

'I'm not rejecting it. As I said, it'll be with me the rest of my days. A beautiful memory to be cherished for ever. Something that has nothing to do with the damn rat race and with having to explain to everybody why after so many years I still don't have a secure job.'

'I don't have much,' she said. 'But my father did leave some money when he died. Why don't you take it and do something with it?'

'I don't know what to do with money.'

'Look, we'll find some way of investing it. Let's just try to be happy as long as we can.'

'That's not possible,' I said. My jaw still ached from the lifeguard's blows. There was a buzz in my head and I couldn't concentrate. I couldn't remember what I was supposed to say to her next, and I didn't feel like going down to the lobby and phoning Robert. I remembered seeing a huge gorilla of a man that morning lying on the beach watching little Johnny. I imagined Johnny playing some prank and the gorilla losing his temper and going after me. I shuddered. I heard my rasping breath in the darkness; I got up, turned on the light, and approached the mirror. I leaned my forehead against the glass but got no relief; the mirror was warm and slippery.

'Go to your room,' I said.

'I won't leave you alone now.'

'Go away, I want to sleep. This is all so incredibly stupid, and the wind is getting on my nerves. Go to hell. I don't want you or the money your father left you. I moved into this hotel to con you out of some money; Robert was going to help me. Some other things were to happen, too, but I'm glad it's all over now.' I turned away from the mirror and closed my eyes, but the instant I did that, I saw the gorilla coming at me, his jaw clenched in fury. I opened my eyes and met her stare; the expression on her face was both amused and watchful. 'I've hustled other women before,' I said. 'But now I've had enough. Not that I've become more sensitive all of a sudden, or that I want to reform. I'd be happy to live this way for a thousand years. But I don't feel too well today. I'll be going to Tveriah next, together with Robert, where we'll try to swindle some other girl. I have no plans to leave for Australia. I don't even know where it is.'

She laughed. 'Why don't you tell me that you have a wife and kid, and that's why you need money?'

'I don't have any kids. I've spent more money on abortions than there is in the Vatican budget. Even though I'm careful. As you've probably noticed.' I went over and sat on the bed.

'Easy,' she said. 'Easy. It'll pass. It's all because of this wind. Don't talk. There's no need to talk. I'm here with you.'

She put her arms so tightly around me I couldn't move. The silence was total: I could hear the slow, painful beating of my heart and her quiet whispering. This was probably how she had spoken to Johnny when he was very small and had trouble falling asleep. I think God created her so that she would give men love, peace and rest. So that she could make them tired and then make them sleep. I'm sure He forgave her everything.

'I'm just a cheap gigolo,' I said. 'It's not my fault if you don't want to believe me.'

'You're a big boy who probably started shaving too soon,' she said. 'In America you'll buy yourself a sports car and wreck it. I'll help you do it. Now go to sleep. Sleep in peace. It's all because of the wind.'

I didn't answer. I didn't know what to say; I had spoken my own lines, departed from Robert's script. I didn't know how to continue. Robert would have been able to advise me, but he wasn't there. Lying next to her, I tried to imagine her face in the darkness. It was very pleasant to lie like that, totally still, and imagine her face, her good and pretty face, which I would have been able to see if I turned on the light. But I didn't turn it on; I lay

205

next to her, motionless, thinking of her face; then I thought of her soft sloping belly and the small, light scars she had from giving birth to Johnny. She smelled the way a woman should, with a smell resembling the aroma of ripe corn, gentle and strong. There was nothing it could be compared to; and now the bed and this small, dark room were permeated with it. I moved my hand slowly down her flat, warm belly; she clasped my hand between her thighs and now, with the sheet thrown back, her aroma became more intense. When she leaves this room in the morning, I thought, her smell will disappear after a time, though it would be so much nicer if this room and this city retained her smell for ever; then I would always remember she was with me once and life would somehow be more bearable; maybe I would think about her in Tveriah, my next destination, or even years from now, lying in bed with some other woman.

I should have told her all this. I wouldn't have needed Robert and his bloody instructions to do it either. There was so much I could have told her about myself and my life, but she probably wouldn't have believed me. I could have told her how I robbed someone when I was fifteen and wasn't caught. And how three months later a friend and I robbed a ticket office at a train station; my friend was arrested, and I gave myself up so we could go to jail together, because I enjoyed his company. But she wouldn't have believed me. Nor would she believe me if I told her I lost my virginity at the age of twelve to a ripe German girl on the day of her engagement to a young lieutenant. Nor would she believe me if I told her about the German soldier who set his dog on me and then started kicking me and broke my nose just because I wanted to play with the dog – this happened when I was seven. Nor would she believe me that in 1944, in Warsaw, I saw six Ukrainians rape a girl from our building and then gouge her eyes out with a teaspoon, and they laughed and joked doing it. Maybe I myself didn't believe all this any more. I should have told her that I bear the Germans no grudges for killing my family and a few more million Poles, because afterward I lived under the Communists and came to realize that by subjecting men to hunger, fear, and terror, one can force them to do anything under the sun, and that no group of people is better than any other. Those who claim otherwise belong to the lowest human species and their right to live should be revoked.

I should have told her: Listen, I'm just a fucking Polack, and I should have told her my life hadn't prepared me for any other way of living, that none of my experiences would ever come in handy, just as I myself was of no use to anyone, unable to offer any good or any worthwhile advice, because no one would ever believe me if I tried to. And that's the truth. But I didn't say these things. I lay next to her and the warmth of her body enveloped me and put me to sleep, and there was nothing else I wanted to feel or think about.

It would have been a relief to tell her everything. It would have been a relief just to tell her about the Jewish family hiding next door until they were murdered by the Germans. A man, a woman and three children: when their bodies were lying on the ground, the Germans stopped some men walking by and ordered them to piss on the corpses; a German called me over and I pissed, too, shaking with fear, while the Germans photographed the living profaning the dead. And it would have been a relief to tell her how one day, when I was walking to school, the Germans blocked off the street and made us watch them hang people from balconies; no one moved or screamed, not those forced to watch, nor those who were being hanged. But how was I to tell her that? I didn't know. How could I tell her about the girl who fell in love with a German soldier, and, although she had done no one any harm, one day members of the underground caught her, pushed an empty half-litre vodka bottle up her vagina and broke it; she died a few days later. I could have also told her about the Jewish mothers in 1943 who threw their babies into a raging fire, first lifting them high over their heads as if in a gesture of triumph, while Poles made funny remarks from the other side of the ghetto wall. But I think she would have asked me to shut up after my very first words. I tried to tell these things to lots of people, but I don't think anyone ever listened seriously.

I pulled the sheet off her and turned on the lamp. She slept as calmly and peacefully as a child. Her belly was brown, with a golden thread of hair going up from her pubes. Her legs were a bit on the heavy side, her breasts small; dressed up in lace she would have been the perfect model for somebody forging Renaissance portraits. The minute scars on her belly were almost invisible, and I could barely feel them under my fingertips. Suddenly she opened her eyes and her hands began moving, quietly and slowly, waking my desire. And she asked softly, 'You will come with me, won't you?'

208

'No,' I said.

I woke about two hours later. She was no longer in the room. Once again I started to think of the gorilla on the beach and what he would do to me. With the tip of my tongue I could feel the roof of my mouth was swollen. The lifeguard had a forceful punch. Tomorrow it'll really be swollen, I thought; I'll have to go to the dentist and ask him to cut the swelling open. I'll have to sit in his waiting-room for at least an hour and listen to all the other patients tell sickening stories of their own dental problems.

Everything seemed frightening and unbearable. The world was a dark, stinking alley, which I would have to wander in for ever. I felt as if I'd entered the nightmare of a madman or a drunk. I told myself it was all because of the wind, but that didn't help. I had the premonition something tragic was about to happen, but I didn't know where to run or to hide.

I put on my clothes and went downstairs. The hotel clerk was sleeping with a newspaper over his face and I had to shake him by the shoulder several times before he woke up.

'How much do we have to pay?' I asked.

'Are you leaving right now, sir?'

'Tomorrow. How much is it?'

'For yourself only, or for you and the other gentleman?'

'Both of us.'

He started checking his books, but couldn't get the right sum straight away; he would add something first,

209

then subtract, then add again, but finally he said, 'A hundred and thirty pounds. Will you and the other gentleman be staying for breakfast?'

'Yes.'

'Then it'll be a hundred and thirty-five.'

'Okay.'

'Your friend has already paid a hundred pounds. So you only have to pay thirty-five.'

No way we can leave the hotel now, I thought. There's too much to lose; since Robert already put down the money we got from the bouncer, we have to go on with the hustle. Otherwise the bouncer will follow us to hell to get the money we owe him.

I looked at my watch: it was one o'clock. I left the hotel and started walking towards the city. I knew what I planned was stupid and senseless, but I went on anyway. At a certain point a cat with its tail held almost straight up began to follow me along the dark streets. I entered the building where Azderbal lived. I knocked, but nobody opened the door. The cat watched me from the darkness with its honey-brown eyes.

I turned the doorknob and went in. I crossed to the empty dining-room; so did the cat. I went into the bedroom and switched on the light. Azderbal wasn't there; only his girlfriend, and she was a heavy sleeper. I sat on the bed next to her, trying to gather my thoughts and decide why I'd come here. Then I remembered the bouncer who'd invested in us, the gorilla waiting for me at the beach, and also Johnny's father, who would probably knock me out with one blow. I looked at the cat who sat devotedly at my feet.

'Come here, Stanislaw,' I said to the cat, and it jumped on my lap. The girl woke up and lay there staring at us. 'His name is Stanislaw,' I told her.

'What do you want?'

'Money,' I said. 'I intend to sell Stanislaw to you. Where is that he-man of yours?'

'He's gone to Haifa.'

'When will he be back?'

'In two days.'

'I can't wait that long. You have to give me two hundred and thirty pounds. Once you do, Stanislaw is yours.'

'Why did you come to me?'

'Because I'm crazy. And so are you. Who do you think I should have gone to?'

'And if I refuse to buy Stanislaw?'

'You'd better not. Or I'll force you.'

She got up from the bed and went to the mirror. She tidied her hair; watching her I could swear she wanted to make herself look attractive not only for me but for Stanislaw, too.

'Would you like a drink?'

'I wouldn't mind some brandy,' I said. 'Do you have any in the fridge?'

'Why don't you check?'

I went to the refrigerator and took out a bottle of brandy and some fish for Stanislaw. Then I returned to the bedroom and poured a glass for each of us.

'How much do you need?' she asked me after a moment.

'Two hundred and thirty pounds,' I said. 'That includes tomorrow's breakfast. I have to pay for my hotel.'

'So far you've always moved out without paying the bill and it never bothered you. Once you even left a girl behind and she had to pay. I was that girl, remember?'

'That's not a bad idea. Why didn't I think of it earlier? I'll do what you say.'

'You need the money for some woman. There's a woman involved, isn't there?'

'Yes.'

'And you don't want to play a dirty trick on her.'

'I can't just move out,' I said. 'Robert's already paid for the hotel. And it wasn't our money. We have to pay back what we owe or we'll be in trouble.'

'Come off it. You're never in trouble. Even if a hundred women refuse to give you money, you still always find one.'

The cat finished eating the fish and meowed. I got up, took out another fish from the fridge, and gave it to him.

'Poor old male whore,' she said, staring at me. 'Has to go chasing around in the night while everybody else sleeps, and no one will give him any money.'

'You will,' I said. 'Would you like another drink?'

'Yes, please.'

We drank some more brandy. I stared at her legs and realized that she was still quite pretty.

'Five years ago you must have looked like a fresh flower,' I said. 'Did you wear white dresses?'

'Yes.'

'Do you still have them?'

She went to her wardrobe and took one out.

'Nobody wears long dresses any more,' she said. 'They've gone out of fashion.'

'Put it on.'

She stared at the dress for a moment, then threw it on the bed. She sat down at the table and poured herself half a glass.

'Do you still drink as much?' I asked.

'And you?'

'I can't afford it. Anyway, Robert hates alcohol.'

'So what do you do with the money you score?'

'Nothing much. We go to the cinema. Robert eats a lot. Our expenses are high.'

'I only have a hundred pounds,' she said. 'I'll give it to you.'

She took five twenties out of her purse and handed them to me. I put them in my pocket.

'Wait,' she said. 'I forgot something.'

She stretched out her hand and I gave her the notes back. She threw them on the floor, and bent down and spat on them.

'You can take them now. They're all yours.'

I leaned over and picked up the notes. When I looked at her, she burst into tears and flung herself on the bed.

'Go away,' she said after a while.

So I did.

As I walked back along the empty streets, I could tell the wind had changed direction. The sky over the sea was beginning to pale, which made me feel a little better. I knew the khamsin would stop blowing soon. I was about to turn towards my hotel when suddenly I remembered my friend the hunchback who had trouble sleeping at night, too, and was probably sitting in front of the toilet in the hotel on Allenby Road. I felt like talking to him, so I climbed up the stairs and tiptoed past Harry, who was sleeping with a detective novel in his hand. I glanced at the cover; it was the one where Mike Hammer shot his girlfriend in the belly with his ·45. I had read it in prison. Mickey Spillane's novels weren't allowed in jail, and for that reason they were the most popular books there. I remembered I had to pay three or four cigarettes for reading that one.

The hunchback was sitting in his usual spot.

'I can't sleep,' I said.

'You're telling me?'

'Do you have any sleeping pills?'

He raised his eyebrows. 'You're the one who should have them. Or have you quit your profession?'

I looked at my watch. 'Four o'clock. Too late to take any pills. I'd need at least six hours to sleep them off.'

'How's business?'

'Fine. How about your priests? Did they give you the money?'

'Yes. Last night. They also gave me a book about missionaries. I'm reading it now. I've just found out that the most missionaries ever murdered were in China.'

'Listen, do you still want a girl? I have an idea.'

'What?'

'Come with me. You won't have to pay anything.'

He looked doubtful. 'You mean it?'

'Of course. We'll play a complicated joke on somebody.'

214

'Wait. I'll just take some charcoal pills. My bloody stomach . . .'

When we arrived at Azderbal's apartment, the lights were already out. The hunchback slipped quickly into her bed, and I left. I woke around eleven, feeling much better. I thought of the girl; she must have had a terrible hangover and a hunchback was just what she needed in the 105° heat. Then I decided I wouldn't split the money she'd given me with Robert, and my mood improved even more. I'm always sublimely happy when I hit on a scheme to con a partner. Nothing can quite compare with that state of bliss and contentment. I showered and went downstairs for breakfast, bowing to all the ladies I met on the way. I ordered four scrambled eggs. Robert looked sleepy and pale and had big circles under his eyes; sharing a bed with the bouncer wasn't the most comfortable way to spend the night. After breakfast we walked out to the beach. Azderbal's girlfriend must have wakened by then and discovered it wasn't me who had returned in the middle of the night to cover her with caresses. God knows what is really funny.

In the afternoon we took the bus to Jaffa. Robert knew a fellow there who had a dog for sale, but somehow we couldn't find him. We went to a café we knew he frequented and ordered coffee. The man finally appeared and said he'd get the dog.

'You know something, Robert?' I said after the man left. 'Last night I forgot my lines and since you weren't there, I made them up myself.'

'What did you tell her?'

'I told her it's all an act, that we're after the money.'

215

'You didn't!' he exclaimed, turning pale.

'I did. But don't worry, she didn't believe me. It came out beautifully. I'll always do that from now on.'

Robert sat motionless, not saying anything.

'You're upset because it was my idea. Come on, Bobby. Admit it. You're jealous.'

'You could have ruined everything.'

'But I didn't. Why, it only improved my psychological make-up. I'm a complicated and unhappy person, my pride is hurt, interpret it any way you want.'

'Did you tell her everything?'

'Enough.'

'Did you tell her about the girl from Boston?'

'No.'

'You didn't tell her she committed suicide?'

'No.'

'You should have told her everything. That first she had to be locked up in a nuthouse and that a year later . . .'

'I don't like to talk about it.'

'Then don't talk about it at all. Look, I haven't forgotten what kind of person you are. A man at odds with himself, even slightly unbalanced, but the idea that you could take money from a woman should be so abhorrent to you it shouldn't even cross your mind. The way I present you is different and much more modern. Don't forget the times we live in. I show you only in those situations which are essential to your character – when you're in despair, in love, or seething with fury. The rest she can fill in herself. Look how Americans make films. They show only the key situations, the most important

216

ones which move the action forward, and that's why it's all so convincing.'

'Then you have to come up with some new lines for me. There's something missing from my performance, Robert. There's a vacuum at one point. I felt this yesterday, and that's why I departed from the script. Just after I refuse her offer to take me to the States – I don't know how to go on.'

'At this point you should play a man at peace with himself. You've made up your mind. You're like a man condemned to death being led to the firing squad, a man fully in control of his senses who knows this is the end. Understand? Ask her to tell you something about America, ask about unimportant details, like the price of ice cream or the speed limit in California. This should lead up to the climax in which no words are necessary and which must work perfectly.'

I lowered my eyes. 'Okay.'

But he went on with the lecture and I had only myself to blame; I should have known better than to tell him the truth. Once he started on his favourite subject, there was no shutting him up.

'You have no sense of timing and that's bad. And you don't see the whole act, just the separate scenes. I've read that Marlon Brando said an actor has to also be a poet. There's wisdom in that. Brando is always in command of all the material and it shows. The principle you have to base your performance on is very simple, really; if you're locked up in a dark room, you become accustomed to the darkness after a while. But if someone keeps turning the light on and off, your suffering is unbearable, because each time you've got to get used to the light and darkness. That's why when you tell her you won't go to America you have to follow with a period of peace, of quiet. You're both aware that the problem remains, but you're afraid to broach it so as not to hurt each other's feelings. It's like the moment of quiet before a storm, a silence terrible to bear. Haven't you ever read books about the sea and sailors?'

'No,' I said. 'As a kid I only read Ken Maynard's adventures, slim paperbacks that we devoured in class, hidden under our desks.'

'Where did you go to school?'

'In Warsaw. A school run by nuns,' I added quickly, eager to change the subject. 'I was a rotten student. One nun came up with the idea of making a dunce's cap and I had to wear it for almost four years.'

'She must have been a sadist.'

'All of them were. When the bishop of Warsaw diocese died, the kids from Catholic schools had to go and pray for him. There he was, laid out in state, one gloved hand hanging limply from the open coffin, and we had to kneel down and kiss that cold, rigid hand. When my turn came, I said I won't do it, and the nuns dragged me over by force. So I bit into that dead hand with such a fury that it took several nuns to pry me off. They almost overturned the coffin.'

'How old were you?'

'I don't remember. Maybe nine.'

'It's a good story,' Robert said. 'Tell it to that woman. Americans love analysing experiences like that. Let her exercise her brains. A small thing, but what joy it can bring to a woman! Just like a prick.'

The man returned with his dog, a boxer. Both of them looked like cheats. Robert started bargaining with the man while I played with the dog. It was very thin; we knew we'd have to fatten it up before going to Tveriah. The problem was we had nowhere to cook. Oh well, I thought, we can always move back to the hotel on Allenby Road and borrow an electric hotplate from somebody. Maybe even Harry would agree to cook meals for the dog if we paid him extra.

'What's it called?' I asked.

'Call it anything you like,' the man answered. 'It's yours.'

'Not yet,' Robert answered. 'We haven't bought it yet. This isn't a dog, it's skin and bones. What have you been feeding it? Barbiturates?'

'This is a pedigree. Pedigrees shouldn't be fat. Just like good fighting cocks.'

'We'll pay you eighty pounds for the dog, but you'll have to keep it three or four days longer. Here, fifty pounds in advance, but be sure you take good care of it.'

'Who said I'd sell it for eighty pounds?'

'I did.'

They started arguing again. I turned away and studied the street. There was everything a man could ever need: army jeeps, mules, girls, soldiers, Arabs, whites; the street smelled of hot copper and spicy foods, mules, haircream, sea breeze, and petrol; now, at six in the evening, the shadow of two slim minarets fell across it. I regretted Robert was about to wind up the deal and we would have to get back on the crowded bus and return to Tel Aviv. It would have been so much more enjoyable to stay on in the café, order beer, and wait until dusk, when the shadows of the slim minarets would fade and vanish and the charred sky would cover the earth with blackness.

Surprisingly, though, the bus wasn't crowded; apart from Robert and me, there were only several workers, and they fell asleep right away. The driver sped along the narrow streets, then turned towards the sea; at last we felt the fresh breeze that always begins just before the tide turns. The smell of copper, mules, and haircream disappeared. The sea looked cool and bright. The first stars emerged. It crossed my mind that in prayers in Poland to the Holy Virgin, she is often called 'the Morning Star'. I asked Robert whether it could possibly be because another name for the star which shines the longest is the Star of Hope, but he told me to think of Tveriah instead and to find a good name for the dog.

'Its name must be as powerful as thunder,' he said. 'The dog appears on the scene, barks twice, we call out its name, and suddenly everything falls into place. Think of how Dostoyevsky named his characters. Take Dmitry Karamazov. That name is dynamite. There's strength in it, there's truth about human nature, there's everything you could wish for.'

'What do you know about the girl in Tveriah?'

'She's a divorcee. It'll work out well. Her husband turned out not to be the strong, virtuous man she had hoped to marry. He failed to fulfil her dreams and was blind to her sensitive nature. That's why she plunged into an affair with her chauffeur, and when he'd had enough and wanted to back out, she threatened to fire

220

him and spill the beans on him to his wife. The chauffeur had a mental breakdown and ended up in a psychiatric clinic; the woman's husband had to pay the bills. And now you'll walk into her life.'

'Bullshit,' I said. 'Who can afford a chauffeur in America these days?'

'Her husband is shortsighted. He can't watch films or read books. And he didn't pay the chauffeur full wages. Don't worry.'

'I wish this would end. Why did I have to be born so fucking poor?'

'And me?'

The bus slowed down. 'Your stop,' the driver called out to us over his shoulder.

We got out.

'I know what we can call the dog,' I said to Robert. 'What?'

'Loser. It'll be like a paradoxical reaction. The last time I was in the hospital there were some patients who were trying to kick their addiction to sleeping pills. They suffered terribly. To fall asleep, just before bedtime, they had to drink giant mugs of strong black coffee. It's what the doctors call a paradoxical reaction. It'll be the same with the new dog. It's fine-looking, it'll eat for two, so the name should work. What do you think?'

'Okay. From time to time you'll allude to the dog when you're talking to her. Subtly, of course. I'll tell you how.'

'Yes,' I said. 'You know best.'

In the evening we sat down to dinner: Robert, me, and little Johnny. A sickening family atmosphere prevailed in this hotel; I had to pass the time of day with these loafers and participate in conversations about food, the weather, and the beauty of the land. It was simply awful; Robert was much better at small talk. He could discuss any topic for hours.

'Where's your mother?' I asked the kid.

'Go to hell,' he said, then added: 'She's making herself look beautiful. As if you didn't know.' He turned to Robert. 'Has he always been this dumb?'

Robert interrupted the conversation he was having with some old geezer who, by the looks of him, should have been long dead. 'Yes, my dear?' Robert asked.

'Nothing,' Johnny said. 'You're just as dumb as he is.'

The guests at the next table burst out laughing. I flushed red and got up abruptly, walked over to the lift, and pressed the button. Someone from the next table, a man in his early fifties with the contented look of a gangster who has made enough money to give up crime and turn into an honest citizen, joined me at the lift.

'That kid sure made a fool of you,' he said.

'Is that what you think?' I pushed him into the lift and walked up the stairs. I opened the door to her room; she was sitting on the bed with an unlit cigarette in her hand.

'Don't you feel well?' I asked.

'Not really.'

'What's wrong?'

'Nothing. Except Johnny's father is coming here tonight.'

'How do you know?'

'He called to ask whether it'd be okay. I told him yes.'

'It'll turn out all right, don't worry. Light your cigarette and come downstairs with me.'

222

'You think it will?'

'I'm certain.'

'You don't know what it means to Johnny to actually meet his father. It's all my fault, of course. It was me who kept telling him how wise and strong his daddy was; I said everything he wanted to hear. And now he believes everything I told him and expects to meet some superman.'

'I don't see how you can change that at this point.'

'I know. But Johnny is too young to understand. He's expecting a strong, wonderful stranger to come up to him and say: "John, my son, I'm your daddy."'

'And what's your ex-husband really like?'

'I'm not sure. But he's not what Johnny's been dreaming about.' Suddenly she burst into tears and cried just like that time on the beach, hopelessly and unobtrusively, as a child might. 'I didn't want Johnny to suffer. Or feel unloved. What else could I do?'

'Come on, let's go,' I said. 'It'll be okay.'

She looked up at me and smiled. 'You really think so?'

'Remember, I'll be there. And so will Uncle Robert. And the dog.'

We went downstairs. The reformed gangster I had met at the lift sent me a murderous look. I sat down.

A strange calm descended over me, as it sometimes does. As soon as the man walked into the dining-room, I knew what was going to happen. He recognized me immediately: it was that poor wino who had asked Robert for a beer and who I'd chased away. He was more drunk than before and there was a foolish grin on his face; he must have wanted to muster up his courage.

Then he saw me; I had no doubt what he'd do. As the memory of our previous meetings stirred in his unhappy, intoxicated mind, his grin vanished. He came up to us, bumping into the waiter serving soup to the guests sitting at the next table; the soup landed right in their laps.

'You whore,' he said to her.

I got up. 'Is that the way to greet a lady?' I asked.

'Whore,' he said again.

She clutched my hand.

We looked at each other, and at that moment he must have understood everything. It became very quiet. He hit me in the face and two women screamed. I grabbed him by the throat, but then I saw the expression on the kid's face. He was watching me, pale and frightened; his nose wrinkled like a dog's, his upper lip curled, showing his teeth.

I didn't say anything, just pushed the drunk away, or, rather, let go of him, and he staggered and almost fell. A deep silence descended over the room. I started walking towards the door, tossing away a napkin I had unconsciously picked up from the table. When the door slammed behind me, pandemonium broke out.

Robert caught up with me on the stairs. His face was pale and covered with sweat.

'Now,' he said. 'Don't wait, do it now. Everything came out beautifully, it'll be just perfect.'

'No, not today,' I said. 'Tomorrow.'

He kissed my hand; I could feel his lips trembling. 'You were wonderful, magnificent! But don't wait, do it now. Tomorrow won't be the same.'

'Okay.'

We went into the room. Robert took out the pistol from our suitcase and started loading it. His hands were shaking. I walked up to the window and gazed at the sea. Robert kept talking, but I wasn't listening. I was watching our dog run around on the beach; some kids were chasing it, and it was barking loudly.

'Ready,' Robert announced.

I turned round and took the pistol from him.

'Just don't hit me too hard,' he said.

'Have I ever hit you too hard?'

'No. You were fantastic, fantastic. Let's go.'

'I want to look at the sea again.'

'There's no time.'

We started going down the stairs. At the bottom landing I broke into a run; Robert followed me with great strides.

'It's madness!' he screamed. 'Stop him!'

I was supposed to hit him, but I only pushed him away. I crossed the dining-room and ran out to the beach. There was a strong wind blowing, so the beach was practically deserted. I whistled, and Spot began running towards me in huge leaps; I pulled the trigger, firing several times in rapid succession, but I didn't manage to empty the gun. The dog lay sprawled at my feet. It must have been dead after the second or third shot. I threw the gun next to the body and went back to my room.

Three bottles of Nembutal were waiting for me on the table. I took the glass of water Robert had prepared for me and started swallowing the pills. Robert was scribbling something; drops of perspiration fell onto the sheet of paper.

'What are you writing?' I asked.

''Pray for my soul,'' he said.

'Better write: ''Forgive me my sins and pray for my miserable soul.'' And maybe add: ''None of you ever truly liked me, nor did I ever truly like any of you.''

'No. Only this: ''Pray for my soul.'' It's more forceful.'

I stretched out on the bed and said, 'Leave me now.'

'Do you feel anything?'

'Not yet. But I will soon. Go away.'

He stood hesitating.

'Go away,' I said again.

'Okay. So long, son. In two days' time it'll be all over. Don't worry.'

He left. I knew I would feel a rocking for a while, and I did. I was being carried by some dark and gentle wave, but I didn't fall asleep at once. I knew the next moment would be the worst; I always dreaded it.

I was no longer in a cheap and ugly hotel room. I was no longer carried by a gentle wave. I was walking along a country road and I could see in the distance, in the middle of an empty field, a girl with her back to me; I could see her long hair, her beautiful slender legs and her tanned shoulders. She was bending over something hidden from my sight, which I knew I would never see. Then I suddenly found myself back in my bed in the tastelessly decorated hotel room, but in the next moment I was looking at the girl's graceful figure again. I knew I would see her face now.

'Don't be shy,' I said aloud. 'I'm coming to you.'

She turned to me, and I saw her face, old and ugly, then she smiled, exposing her rotten teeth. I could even smell her awful, stinking breath. I knew I was already on the other side of the hill.

On the third day it was all over. I was lying on the terrace of a small, elegant hotel, pretending to be asleep. It was very quiet because everybody was resting after dinner, so I had no trouble hearing what Robert was telling her. I knew his text almost by rote, but I enjoyed listening to him all the same.

'At least he'll have enough sleep,' Robert said. 'He often suffers from insomnia.'

'What do you think? Should I leave now?' she asked. 'I'm afraid he may feel embarrassed when he wakes up.'

'He should,' Robert said, and I knew there was a stern look on his face, just as if he were playing the part of an Indian chief sending somebody to his death. 'It's no joke. Whatever one does, one has to try to do it right.'

'Don't be so cruel.'

'Poor, stupid loser. He even failed to take his own life.'

'He would have died if you hadn't gone back to the room,' she said.

'Yes, that was sheer luck. I'd forgotten to take my passport and I needed it the next day. I didn't want to wake the two of you in the morning.'

They both fell silent for a moment.

'That poor dog was all he had,' Robert said. 'I don't know why he shot it. Maybe he had to get his anger out after your husband hit him. So he shot the dog.'

'He shouldn't have done it.'

'Thank God he did!'

'Why?'

227

'Because he fired all the bullets he had, so he couldn't shoot himself. All that remained were those stupid sleeping pills.'

'To kill himself because of that worthless drunk!'

'No. It was because your son was present. The kid saved his father. Jacob didn't want to hit him because of the kid.'

'I know. Someday Johnny'll understand.'

'Write to him,' Robert said. 'He'll be happy to hear from you.'

'Write?'

'Yes. Send the letter to me and I'll forward it to him.'

'But he's coming with me!'

'I'm afraid you don't know him,' Robert said.

'Listen, there's something wrong here. Something I don't understand. Why does he have to go to Australia to work? Why can't he come to America with me and try to find a job there? I don't get it, Bobby.'

'It's simple. He's scared.'

'Of what?'

'I don't know if I can tell you.'

'Bobby, you're the only friend he has. If you won't help me, who will? Bobby, please!'

'His isn't a romantic story, it's a sad one,' Robert said. 'Have you seen the picture of an old lady in his room?'

'You mean his mother?'

'Yes,' Robert said, and I remembered the snapshot of the bouncer's mum. 'She was very ill and he had to go into debt to send her money for the hospital and the operation. Unfortunately, it didn't do much good. She died.'

'Oh, the poor man,' she whispered, and the image of my real mother, who is in perfect health and swills vodka like a hussar, flashed through my mind.

'He can't leave Israel without his passport, and it's held by the lawyer representing the people he borrowed money from. When he told the lawyer he'd found employment in Australia and showed him his contract, the lawyer agreed to return the passport. But the arrangement is that Jacob's Australian employer will regularly deduct part of his pay and send it directly to the creditors. Do you see it all now?'

'Why can't he send them money from the States?'

'Because he's a Pole, dear,' Robert said, 'and he'd have to wait six or eight years for an immigration visa. He can go to the States as a tourist only. And to go as a tourist you need money.'

'How much does he owe these people?'

'Two thousand three hundred and eighty dollars.'

'Do you mean to tell me he wanted to kill himself for two thousand dollars?'

'I didn't say that was the reason. I can only guess what went on in his mind. He finally managed to find a job and then he met you. He didn't want to go to Australia any more, only to the States with you. But that damned lawyer wouldn't let him have his passport. Next your husband showed up and hit him in the face, and he couldn't hit him back because of your kid. So he shot the dog and his mind went crazy. I don't know what really happened. You're the one who should know.' His voice was stern and hard.

After a moment, she asked softly, 'Why, Bobby? Why do you think I should know?'

229

'Because he loves you,' Robert replied in the same stern voice. 'And you love him.'

'Will you hate me if I take him away?'

'No. It's me who's a loser. I don't hate anybody.' He paused and said again, 'Yes, I'm a loser.'

'Do you know how to straighten things out with that lawyer?'

'He has to go to him to pay off his debts.'

'Oh, God, he won't do it. He won't take money from me.'

Robert was silent for a long while, then he laughed.

'What are you laughing at, Bobby?'

'At myself. We've been friends for so long and gone through so much together. And yet the only thing I can do for him is to help him leave, even though it means I'll never see him again. Isn't that something? But I'll do it.'

Neither of them said a word for a while. I couldn't see the sea from the terrace, but I could hear the waves. They had kicked us out of the hotel, and we were all staying in a small inn owned by a German Jew, a calm, elderly gentleman with well-groomed hands. Robert had brought me there from the hospital earlier in the day. He had to sign a statement saying that the patient was being released at his own request and against medical advice. And so here I was, and next to my bed was a vase full of flowers. I amused myself by imagining Robert's expression when he'd bought them for me.

'Will you make us some coffee, Bobby?' she said.

'Okay, but if you want, we can go downstairs for coffee.'

'Bobby, I still don't understand why he shot his dog.'

230

'I don't know,' he said. 'I think he intended to destroy everything he possessed. Or maybe he wanted to make the parting with you easier for himself? I don't know. The dog was his. It was all he had.'

'I'm wondering how to explain it to Johnny. You know, Bobby, that all Americans love dogs?'

'Tell him Spot was ill and had to be shot. In Westerns cowboys often shoot their horses and everybody thinks that's all right. When he grows up, you can tell him Jacob shot the dog because he was in love with you and thought he'd have to leave you. So he shot the dog to appear cruel and stupid. So you wouldn't have to suffer, you know.'

'Is that true, Bobby?' 'Let's go and have coffee,' he said.

'Why am I so dumb?' she cried. 'Why didn't I think of it myself? He killed the dog because he wanted me to stop loving him, didn't he, Bobby?'

'Let's go have that coffee.'

'I should have thought of it myself.'

'You'll have lots of time to think it all through,' he said. 'I can promise you that. Come on, let's go. I need that coffee.'

I turned over and went to sleep.

They were leaving the next day. After breakfast I rang for a taxi and picked up her suitcase to carry it down to the lobby.

'No,' she said, taking it out of my hand. 'You're still too weak.'

'I won't say good-bye to you,' I said.

'Why not?'

'There's a saying that welcomes are nicer than farewells.'

She stood in front of me, smiling, then she turned and climbed into the waiting cab. 'John would like to speak to you,' she said through the window.

'Will it be very painful?'

'Who knows?'

I turned; the kid was standing behind me, solid as a rock. Robert was arguing with the taxi-driver over the fare.

'You wanted to talk to me?' I asked.

'Yes,' Johnny said. 'But not here. Let's go somewhere.'

We moved away from the cab. But he didn't say anything; he just stared gloomily at his plimsolls.

'What's the problem, Johnny?'

'Listen,' he said, jerking his head up, 'I know you could have smashed my daddy to bits.'

'Is that so?'

'I know you could have made him spit chalk. And I know why you didn't.'

'Did your mum tell you?'

'Nobody had to tell me anything. I'm not dumb. Mom didn't tell me anything, by the way.'

'Okay. Consider the matter closed. Thank you, John.'

But he hadn't finished yet. I saw tears in his eyes; I knelt down and embraced him, and he threw his arms around my neck.

'I'd like to ask you something,' he said.

'Go ahead, ask anything you want.'

'When you come to the States, can I call you Daddy?'

232

'Yes,' I said. 'You can start calling me that now.'

He left, and as soon as he climbed into the cab, it drove away. Precisely at this moment the bouncer appeared, as suddenly as if he had emerged from under the ground. I'll never know where he had been hiding so well that nobody saw him, neither Robert, nor me, nor her. He was beaming; he looked like a potato blessed with intelligence.

'Okay,' he said. 'Now we can settle our accounts.'

He and Robert sat down; so did I, but I didn't listen to them. A group of young women in uniform were walking down Yarkon Street singing. I watched them for a while, and then turned back to the two men. When I did, my share of the money was waiting for me; I pocketed the bills without counting. Robert and the bouncer were arguing again about an earlier deal.

'Where did you go?' Robert asked.

'I went to see J.'

'J. knew nothing of this scheme. I told you to go and see G.'

'I won't let you order me around.'

'And I won't let you swindle me.'

I remembered it was time to collect our new dog, and since Robert's squabbles usually bored me, I decided to leave him with the bouncer and go to Jaffa by myself. I knew how much Robert enjoyed arguing; now I also knew about the bouncer. As I was slowly walking down Yarkon Street, it crossed my mind that in fact I knew the whole city, the whole country. I passed a nightclub, which was closed at this time of day. I knew the black who played drums there; I thought of his drums covered

233

with dust until evening when his quick fingers would bring them to life with the beat of a song. I passed a small hotel where a queer who was in love with me worked as a desk clerk; whenever I wanted to get money from him, I would cut my face with a razor blade and make him watch. I did this when I was really broke.

I knew many places and many people here. Why couldn't I write about them? Why could I feel so much but not be able to put it down in writing? I don't know. Why haven't I ever said or written that there is no greater misery than living without awareness of God, contrary to His commandments? I don't know. And why haven't I ever said that the worst sin is to betray the love of another human being? I don't know. Maybe it was too hot for such profound statements, or maybe I've forgotten. I had seven hundred American dollars and over a hundred pounds in my pockets. In Israel, seven hundred dollars is a lot of money. And I expected to score some more in Tveriah. I'd be able to rent a separate room for myself, buy lots of books, and read them; evenings I'd go to the cheap cinema on Ben Yehuda Street, and late at night I'd listen to the rain fall on the city. And so it would be till spring. Until spring I wouldn't have to talk of love to anybody; till spring I wouldn't have to hustle any more women. But why did I have to be poor, why wasn't I born in some rich bastard's bed? If I were rich, I could live in solitude among millions of people and share their joys instead of only their exhaustion. Nothing will ever change for me.

I had to get that damn boxer. On the corner of Yarkon sat a poor man who made his living shining shoes. I walked up to him, sat down, and watched his old hands polish my shoes. When he finished, I pulled out a pound note, rolled it into a ball, and tossed it to him.

'God bless you, mister,' he said. 'You're a good man.'

'I like that,' I said. I took another pound note from my pocket, rolled it into a ball and threw it at him. He looked up at me expectantly. 'I like what you said,' I told him. 'In about an hour I'll be coming back this way with a dog. When you see me, say that again, okay?'

A Selected List of Titles Available from Minerva

While every effort is made to keep prices low, it is sometimes necessary to increase prices at short notice. Mandarin Paperbacks reserves the right to show new retail prices on covers which may differ from those previously advertised in the text or elsewhere.

The prices shown below were correct at the time of going to press.

☐	7493 9137 5	**On the Eve of Uncertain Tomorrows**	Neil Bissoondath	£5.99
☐	7493 9050 6	**Women In A River Landscape**	Heinrich Boll	£4.99
☐	7493 9921 X	**An Instant in the Wind**	Andre Brink	£5.99
☐	7493 9147 2	**Explosion in a Cathedral**	Alejo Carpentier	£5.99
☐	7493 9109 X	**Bodies of Water**	Michelle Cliff	£4.99
☐	7493 9060 3	**Century of the Wind**	Eduardo Galeano	£4.99
☐	7493 9080 8	**Balzacs Horse**	Gert Hofmann	£4.99
☐	7493 9093 X	**The Notebook**	Agota Kristof	£4.99
☐	7493 9174 X	**The Mirror Maker**	Primo Levi	£4.99
☐	7493 9143 X	**Parents Worry**	Gerard Reve	£4.99
☐	7493 9172 3	**Lives of the Saints**	Nino Ricci	£4.99
☐	7493 9003 4	**The Fall of the Imam**	Nawal El Saadawi	£4.99
☐	7493 9924 4	**Ake**	Wole Soyinka	£5.99
☐	7493 9139 1	**The Four Wise Men**	Michel Tournier	£5.99
☐	7493 9092 1	**Woman's Decameron**	Julia Voznesenskaya	£5.99

All these books are available at your bookshop or newsagent, or can be ordered direct from the publisher. Just tick the titles you want and fill in the form below.

Mandarin Paperbacks, Cash Sales Department, PO Box 11, Falmouth, Cornwall TR10 9EN.

Please send cheque or postal order, no currency, for purchase price quoted and allow the following for postage and packing:

UK including BFPO	£1.00 for the first book, 50p for the second and 30p for each additional book ordered to a maximum charge of £3.00.
Overseas including Eire	£2 for the first book, £1.00 for the second and 50p for each additional book thereafter.

NAME (Block letters) ....

ADDRESS ....

....

☐ I enclose my remittance for ....

☐ I wish to pay by Access/Visa Card Number

Expiry Date